80 Miles from Nowhere

80 Miles from Nowhere

Melissa Aylstock

CFI
Springville, Utah

ISBN 13: 978-1-55517-896-0
ISBN 10: 1-55517-896-0

Published by CFI, an imprint of Cedar Fort, Inc., 925 N. Main, Springville, UT, 84663
Distributed by Cedar Fort, Inc. www.cedarfort.com

LIBRARY OF CONGRESS CATALOGING-IN-PUBLICATION DATA
Aylstock, Melissa Ann.
  80 miles from nowhere / by Melissa Aylstock.
    p. cm.
  Novel.
  ISBN 1-55517-896-0 (acid-free paper)
  I. Title: Eighty miles from nowhere. II. Title.

PS3601.Y57A614 2006
813'.6--dc22

                                                          2006002148

Cover design by Nicole Williams
Cover design © 2006 by Lyle Mortimer
Printed in the United States of America

10   9   8   7   6   5   4   3   2   1

Printed on acid-free paper

Prologue

Magna est veritas, et praevalibit
(Truth is might and will prevail)

Fort Leonardwood, Missouri, 1982

The young soldier sat on the edge of his bunk, staring blankly at a fly turning and spinning, fighting for an escape from the gossamer web above his bed. The soldier rhythmically kneaded and mangled a piece of parchment, his mouth drawn and dry.

There were only three words on the paper: "I did it." There was no signature, no return address on the envelope next to him—but he knew the handwriting and what had been done.

It was over before it had begun.

He moved slightly and felt his Beretta jab at his right thigh. He absently moved it to a more comfortable position. His dog tags rested on his bare, thin but well-defined chest. He ran one hand over his ultrashort ginger colored hair and knew it was time again to have it cut. It was an unusually hot May, complicated by the barracks' air-conditioning, which didn't work.

He stood and reached toward the soft netting, trying to gently pull the sticky, silky webbing from around the flailing fly. His shaking fingers were too cumbersome to unwind the delicate threads. He sighed and put the black-winged insect out of its misery. It might be too late for the fly, but at least it wouldn't be eaten alive. Then, squishing the resident spider between his freckled thumb and index finger, he bit down hard on his lower lip. A single tear pooled under his right eye.

Chapter

1

Lance crouched at the edge of the highway, chewing on his lower lip, as his truck bled crimson behind him. Glancing back at the gradually expanding puddle of cherry goo under his truck, he shook his head and thrust his hands into the pockets of his cargo shorts.

Not ten minutes before, just on the outskirts of Nevada, he had felt his transmission slip. It had heightened his adolescent car buff senses to the point that found him ignoring the posted freeway signs. He made an illegal U-turn on the gravel turnaround normally used only by the highway patrol, emergency vehicles, and bored teenagers. His initial plan was to limp back to Wendover to check out his 4Runner, but the sudden loss of engine power indicated otherwise. Pulling hard and to the right, he settled his 4Runner on the shoulder of I-80.

The heavy red fluid had drizzled out, leaving a trail down

the westbound lane of I-80 as far as the eye could see. Now it just oozed—the last drops signaling the imminent death of a recently installed transmission. A passing good Samaritan had let him use a cell phone to call for help. It would be another thirty minutes before the tow truck arrived.

Lance looked north and surveyed the salt-encrusted desert before him. He looked south and saw two trains slowly coming toward each other on the other side of the freeway.

The train from the east looked about a mile long and was loaded with auto carriers; the train coming out of Wendover was shorter and looked like an Amtrak.

Hmm, he thought randomly, remembering that series of math questions he hated so much: if a train leaves Salt Lake City heading west at forty-five miles per hour, and a train leaves Wendover heading east at thirty-five miles per hour, how long would it take before the tow truck driver showed up to overcharge him on his way back to town? He had always had a tough time with those kinds of problems.

He looked back to the north; the fragile sea of salt shoreline was littered with flotsam from previous breakdowns: brown beer bottles, black tire shards, cigarette butts, and a too-fresh-to-inspect disposable diaper. The acrid smell of urine assaulted his nose, so he walked out onto the glistening white edge of the Bonneville Salt Flats, the Dopplered sound of the trains behind him. He didn't worry about someone stealing his car; at this point, no one but a tow truck driver could.

Near the shoreline of this virtual sea, the salt crunched and buckled under his slim but muscular frame. Twenty feet in, the salt softened due to recent rains and stuck to the bottom of his Sketchers. One hundred feet in, the salt was so soft and malleable that he could scoop it up and mold it into soft white salt balls—which he did.

Lance amused himself for a while with an imaginary salt ball fight. As he crouched down, dipping into the soft salt to make another ball, his fingers touched something hard and metallic. He instinctively pulled his hand out. Then he carefully pushed his long slender fingers back into the depths of the salt field and felt around for what he had touched. His middle finger bumped it first. His brows met in the center of his face, cornflower blue eyes wandering up as he pondered what he was feeling. He cautiously wiggled his whole hand around the object. It was tangled in plastic, but even so, he could feel the shape of the gun before he pulled it from its sodium grave.

Slowly he retrieved the gun from the salt and muck of the earth. Lifting the weapon gently out, an attached silver chain pulled up the wet salt in a line that snaked for a short distance. A pair of dog tags popped out of the sand and arched freely upon the end of the chain into the air.

The plastic baggie covering the gun had a few holes in it. Salt had seeped in, eating away part of the metallic finish, eroding the gun's outside bluing, though not enough to hide the distinctive shape of a semiautomatic handgun. He wrestled with the thin baggie, and it shredded as it pulled away from the gun. Turning the gun over a few times, he inspected it. Tentatively, he pressed the magazine release and the magazine failed to eject. He grabbed at the magazine and pressed the button again while he pulled at it. It came out under protest. Stamped on the back of the slide was 92F—a Beretta. Cocking the hammer, he gently pulled back the slide and looked into the chamber. Pushing his Oakleys off the bridge of his nose so he could see better, he squinted from the reflected sun. He searched for the distinctive brass of a round. There was none.

Fingering the salt-encrusted dog tags next, he tried knocking off the dirt and crud to read a name, but the naturally occurring element had crystallized on the silver metal, and it would take more than a simple fingernail scratch to reveal the original owner's identity.

He pulled up his six foot one frame and yawned while stretching his sun-freckled arms back and skyward, the chain dangling from the hand that held the gun. Replacing his sunglasses, he considered turning the items in to the police but slowly shook his head toward the hills above Wendover. He bent down and neatly reburied the plastic bag—his answer to being ecologically concerned. After closing the slide and de-cocking the hammer, he shoved the gun and dog tags in the side pocket of his cargo shorts and walked back toward his truck.

Next to his 4Runner, he stamped his feet to get the sticky salt off his shoes. He left crusty white sneaker prints on the asphalt. As he scraped the last of the salt off his shoes, Tip-of-the-Lake Towing pulled up.

A sun-kissed blond kid about Lance's age stepped from the cab, a Redvine hanging from his mouth. He looked at the burgundy fluid under the truck and then at Lance, and said, "Ouch."

"Yeah," Lance agreed.

"Blake." The kid put out a relatively grease free hand and gave him a business card.

"Lance," he said, taking the card and shoving it toward his pocket. It missed completely and fluttered to the ground.

"Nice truck, though. I've got an '86 Toyota short-bed myself."

"Still running, I hope," Lance said.

"Oh, off and on—it's a wheeler. Right now, I'm putting a six-inch lift on, so it's in the garage at home. So man, where do you want to go? It's eight miles back to Wendover and about a hundred to Salt Lake."

"Where do you suggest?

"There's probably more help near Salt Lake than here. There's also Lake Point—they do a lot of repair work there too."

"How far from Lake Point to Salt Lake?"

Blake shrugged his shoulders. "Twenty-five miles."

"I have one hundred miles towing on this card, right?" Lance held out the red and blue plastic card from his parents' insurance company for Blake to see.

"Yeah."

"So where do you suggest I go for my hundred miles?"

The kid looked a little puzzled. "You aren't in a hurry?"

Lance shook his head. "Not really, I just need to get her fixed and back on the road."

Blake noticed the sleeping bag and tent in the backseat of the 4Runner. He nodded toward the back seat. "You on a road trip?"

"Yeah, I was just planning on cruising through the states for a while."

"Right on. Well, do you want it towed to a shop or are you planning on fixing it in the parking lot of a NAPA?"

Lance laughed. "Well, I suppose I could fix it in the parking lot, but my guess is that NAPA would discourage dismantling transmissions in front of their stores."

Blake smiled and pulled two slightly linty Redvines out of his pocket. He offered one to Lance. Lance took it, nodded in thanks, and stuck it in his mouth. Blake walked around the Runner, sizing it up to put it on the flatbed.

"Nice bumpers."

"Thanks. They were a chore to fabricate."

"You did the welding?" Blake asked, impressed.

"Yeah, me and a buddy. I worked at his dad's shop for a while."

"Right on. You know, if you want, you could park it at my place and fix it. I live in Magna, which is something like 80 miles."

"Seriously?"

"It's not much. Me and a couple of guys rent this old farmhouse outside of town, but it has a field we four-wheel in and a big barn we use as a garage."

"You're sure your roommates aren't going to be . . ."

"Heck no!" Blake cut him off mid-sentence. "The worst you'll have to deal with is Jared. He just returned from a mission, and he can be a bit much at times, but you just have to tell him to back off if he bugs you."

"Mission, huh?" Lance nodded his head knowingly.

"Yeah. You Mormon?"

"Used to be," Lance said without a hint of emotion.

"Oh." Blake paused to look at the tall, freckled kid before him. Shrugging his shoulders, he said, "Well, the offer still stands."

"I'll take it. Thanks," Lance said.

"Let's get this loaded then." Blake walked back to his rig and started to work the controls.

Lance watched as the heavy metal deck hit the asphalt. It bounced on the ground, and he felt his pocket vibrate. He touched the broken handgun at his side and for some reason thought about his biological father.

Chapter

2

Enin ran both of her hands through her hair in a rhythmic motion, one after the other. Each time the open fingers splayed through her hair, her dark auburn hair got tighter and tighter against her skull. With one last sweeping motion, she grabbed the short, thick ponytail in one hand and banded it with an elastic tie with the other. She shook her head back and forth and was ready to go.

The only problem was go *where?*

She could go to the mall with Liz, or to the bowling alley with Stephanie. Her mom wanted her to stay home and do laundry (no way), and her brother wanted her to come over and fix dinner for him and his roommates. Last, but not least, she had a geology report due in two days that required at least one trip to the library—but the library in Magna would be closed soon anyway.

She picked up her garage sale *Dukes of Hazard* lunch box

that doubled as her purse. She took pride in the fact that every one of her girlfriends hated it. She left the house.

She threw the metal box on the seat of her Jeep and backed out of the cracked concrete driveway. When she got to the end of the street, her decision to turn away from downtown Magna was based more on the fact that her brother had a field she could four-wheel in, and she was in the mood to play.

Enin turned up the sound on the Pioneer deck. Brian Rhode's smooth, buttery voice floated out of the open Jeep. Her favorite song about a mission in Colorado was playing, and she thought about Ben, the brother she was about to see, who had chosen not to go on his. The hot wind felt good whipping her ponytail around as she drove a little too fast toward the outskirts of town. Her brother lived with a group of guys she had known all her life. No amount of praying on her or her parents' part had been able to change Ben's mind. It had torn the whole family apart, and now Ben lived with some friends outside of town. She was the only one who kept in close contact with him, though her parents tried. He chose not to talk to their parents, or go to church, or even pretend like he cared about the church anymore.

Thankfully, making dinner for Ben and his roommates was easy—they were happy if she made them a box of store brand macaroni and cheese, and anything beyond that would bring proposals of marriage. However, at twenty, she wasn't quite as ready for the whole marriage thing as Liz and Stephanie were. To hear them talk, you'd think it was Enin's celestial duty to marry young and start her family. Enin wasn't antimarriage— not in the least—but the reality was that most boys didn't much care for her tomboy ways.

Pulling in the long driveway, she was not surprised to see her brother out by the barn helping unload a car off Blake's tow truck. Blake often brought his work home with him, and this time it was a nice little raised 4Runner—white, with serious bumpers.

As she braked hard and threw up a cloud of dust, the boys

unloading the truck looked her way. Blake and Ben smiled, and Jared raised his hand toward her. The other boy, some tall, thin, red-headed kid she didn't recognize, just glanced at her and refocused on getting what was obviously his rig off the tow truck. She pulled her lunch box off the seat, waved to the boys, and headed for the kitchen. She was in the mood for stir-fry, and she knew that the guys would have all the ingredients because she left a food list for them each week. She had a standing invitation to cook and did so a couple of times a week on the condition that they kept their cupboards full. Sometimes she would bring Liz and Stephanie to help, but they hated coming out to the farm because all the boys wanted to do was work on cars. She, on the other hand, loved it and, except for her lack of muscle, could almost keep up with the boys wrench-for-oily-wrench. It was probably what kept her connected to Ben, but that was fine with her.

In half an hour, Enin was setting the table for five. She scrounged up three Blue Willow plates she recognized from her childhood and two melamine plates that probably came with the old farmhouse. She didn't even try to locate matching glasses but just set out five cheap, mismatched plastic tumblers that looked like they were rescued from a Deseret Industries pile about to be shipped to some third-world county. She poured ice-cold lemonade in each and walked toward the open kitchen door.

"Dinner," she yelled out the screen toward the barn.

Blake, Ben, and Jared walked toward the house. The new kid was lagging behind in the garage, obviously having to be convinced to come and eat with them. Blake turned back toward the garage and said something to him that Enin couldn't hear, but it must have done the trick because he was now headed toward the house.

"Smells good," Ben said as he pushed the screen door open. Jared followed behind him. They both turned toward the chipped white enamel sink to wash up. Pumping from a large orange container of degreaser prominently displayed on the windowsill, they cleaned up.

Blake pushed the door open next and was followed in by the new kid.

"Enin, this is Lance. He's staying with us a few days," Blake said as he and Lance took the other boys' places at the sink.

"Hi," Enin smiled.

Lance nodded silently.

Sitting at the table, Jared bowed his head and the others followed suit. Jared's long, heartfelt prayer was tolerated by the hungry boys, but as soon as the 'amen' was behind them, they were loading up their plates with rice, beef, and broccoli.

"So what brings you to Utah, Lance?" Enin asked.

"I wasn't really coming *to* Utah; my Runner just broke down here."

"I saw it. Nice bumpers," Enin said.

Lance had a mouthful of food, so he just nodded.

"So where did you say you came from?" Jared asked.

"Sacramento," Lance said after he had swallowed hard.

"Oh, really? One of my companions was from Sacramento. Elder Neilson? Well, you might have known him as Ryan Neilson," Jared said.

"Actually, I lived in Rocklin, not in Sacramento itself."

"Oh. Are you planning on a mission when you get home from your road trip?" Jared said.

"Uh, no. Not really," Lance said.

Enin noticed Lance was rapidly tapping his fork against his lemonade glass.

"I thought Blake said you were LDS," Jared continued, oblivious to Lance's discomfort.

"I, uh . . . used to be. I quit."

Jared laughed. "Quit? You can't quit the Church."

"Leave him alone, Jared," Ben said, the tension at the table starting to rise.

"Hey, I was just trying to . . ."

"Drop it, okay?" Ben said. "So, Enin, what's happening in your life? Any new boyfriends I need to beat up?" Ben tried to redirect the conversation.

"Oh, ha ha, Ben," Enin said, shaking her head at her brother.

"Enin. That's an unusual name," Lance said.

"Oh, you don't know the half of it," Blake said. The boys at the table nodded in agreement.

"What?" Lance said confused.

"Ben and Enin come from, well, a uniquely named family—even by Utah standards," Blake said.

"And?" Lance questioned.

Ben spoke up. "The thing is, my dad's name is Mosiah. You know Mosiah, right?"

"Yeah, I read the Book of Mormon," Lance said begrudgingly and shrugged his shoulders.

"Well, after our parents were married, my mom had a set of twin boys. My dad thought it would be noble to name them 'solid' Book of Mormon names, something about 'sons of Mosiah'—a little play on words. I suppose it could have been part of his way of carrying on a family tradition. Anyway, in our family you have—" Ben began to count on his fingers, "Nephi, Sam, Sariah, Joseph, Lehi, Moroni, me—Benjamin—Mormon, who is Enin's twin, but he died pretty soon after he was born, Enin, and Ammon."

"I don't remember an 'Enin' from the Book of Mormon," Lance said honestly.

"You didn't miss her," Enin said. "I was the ninth child born, and Enin is 'nine' spelled backward. Actually, my middle name is Brittany, and I suppose I could go by that, but it's such a common name now. I kind of like the fact that no one has my name. I think my parents thought Enin sounded like a Book of Mormon name."

"It does," Lance said simply and thought about his own unique Mormon middle name but stayed quiet. "So there are ten of you guys?"

"Nine. Mormon died," said Ben.

"Oh, yeah. Sorry."

Enin and Ben nodded.

"How many in your family?" Enin asked Lance.

"Depends."

"Depends on what?" Enin said, cocking her head toward him.

"When you ask, I suppose." Lance took a breath and said by rote, "My mother died when I was six and my stepdad remarried. I have three half-brothers, and then two stepsisters from the next marriage, but then my stepdad got cancer and died. My stepdad's wife remarried this guy who was Mormon, and they had two more kids who I grew up with, but I don't know how you would categorize them."

"Wow, that's a little complicated," Enin said in amazement. "What about on your dad's side?"

"I don't have a dad," Lance said flatly.

"Oh, everybody has a dad. You didn't just spring up out of nowhere," Enin said.

Lance's face clouded over, and Enin could immediately tell she had gone too far. The group ate the rest of dinner in silence. When Enin was done, she pushed her chair back from the table and said a little too lightly. "So who wants desert?"

"Well, I sure do," Jared said, chipping away at the icy silence.

"Me too," Blake added.

Enin turned to get something out of the freezer. She could feel Lance's hot, angry stares on her back, but she didn't know why he should be mad at her. *Whatever,* she thought. *He might have a cool truck—but what a jerk.*

Chapter

3

Wayne Roy sat on the edge of the unmade bed, chewing on the end of a cigar long since extinguished. Rhythmically polishing his pawnshop Glock calmed him down. The dim blue glow of the television was the only light in the heavily curtained room. A rerun of *Jeopardy* was on. It bugged him that some young, snot-nosed kid from Salt Lake had been on for over a month. He had watched every program, and he figured that someone needed to shoot the jerk and just get on with the show. He pointed his gun at the television; it wasn't fair for him to keep winning all the money.

As much as he hated the program though, he never changed the station. The TV didn't have a remote, and he was usually too comfortable on his bed to get up.

He kicked off his slippers and set the gun on the bed. He was annoyed that he was going to have to put on shoes for the next couple of hours. He hated shoes; they were too confining, and they made his feet hurt. Boots were the worst though—they made his feet sweat, and that made them itch and burn. He eyed his old khaki army boots peeking out from under the TV stand. He thought back to when he first wore them in Desert Storm. He hated them then, and it was no better now—but they did serve a purpose, so he kept his old pair around.

Wayne stood and padded with his large, soft bare feet over to the dusty closet of the hotel room. He bent over to pick up his running shoes, his rolls of mid-line fat collapsing on each other as he did. Grabbing a pair of old socks balled up in a pile of dirty laundry, he shook them out and then put them up against his nose and breathed in. He didn't gag, so they would do.

After he dressed, he pulled open the thick corduroy room-darkening curtains slightly. Grimacing against the light, he rubbed at his eyes. He didn't want to leave the air-conditioned room, but he had to get the stuff back today if he was going to leave tomorrow. He grabbed the keys from the dresser and put them in his right pocket. He put the Glock in the lower pocket of his camo-cargo pants.

A wave of high desert heat slapped him as he opened the door. He hated Nevada. He hated the heat, the gritty dirt, and the constant sun. He wanted to go back to the beach town where he'd grown up—and he would, he assured himself, as soon as he had cleaned up one last thing.

"Afternoon," the motel's dark, leather-skinned gardener said to him as he walked toward his car.

Wayne didn't reply but put the key into the door of the old gray Taurus.

He left the Triple 7 Hotel parking lot and turned east on Wendover Boulevard.

As he headed toward the freeway entrance on the Utah side of town, he noticed two nice looking young girls in rather short skirts standing outside the Montego Bay Casino. He licked his lips unconsciously.

Accelerating onto I-80, his car protested, a high-pitched

whine screeching from the back of the sedan. He ignored it. He was ditching the car in a day or so anyway. Ten miles outside of Wendover, he passed a rest stop. He scanned the freeway before him and then looked in his rearview mirror—no cops. He pulled into the fast lane after a candy apple red Corvette passed him doing about 100 mph. The only cars behind him now were a half-mile back. He slowed down, pulled into the center divide, and then used a highway patrol turnaround and headed west—back toward Wendover. He passed the rest stop again and drove to mile marker 8 where he pulled over and stopped the car.

He wasn't worried about people stopping to help; people seldom did anymore. He got out of the Taurus and walked around the car. Circling the back of the car, he noticed a large, fresh oil slick on the pavement. His lips curled at the thought of someone being stuck in this desert—misery loves company and all. Straddling the puddle, he unlocked his trunk and rooted around for his small army shovel. Turning, he left the pavement for the hardpan of the Bonneville Salt Flats.

He counted off his footsteps. Wayne hadn't gone ten paces before he noticed the semidried footprints in the salt. The footprints stretched toward the northern mountains before him. Tensing, he walked a little faster. Slipping in a random soft spot in the salt, he almost fell forward. He slowed his pace, but not his heart. He followed the footprints until he saw little piles of salt on the desert floor. Someone had been throwing the wet sand around recently, and in the afternoon sun, it had dried into hardened molehills of sodium.

He was so focused on the molehills that he didn't see the larger pile of disturbed salt until he was on it. He stopped now—dead in his salt tracks—and stared. Someone had recently been rooting in the salt—real recent like. Bending down and balancing himself on the small shovel with which he had pierced the salt, large sweat rings formed under his arms; dark circles of damp T-shirt clung to his sides. He took off his pair of cheap sunglasses, wiped at his wet eyebrows, and put them on again.

Cursing, he touched the now-hardening salt. Turning his head, he spit. He pulled the shovel out and gingerly began to move the salt around. He had only made a few loose movements with the shovel when the tip caught on a plastic bag and brought it to the surface. It hung limp in the motionless air. Wayne pulled the bag off the green shovel and frowned. It was his bag—but it was empty.

Reaching toward the ground, he tried to pry the dense salt chunks loose with his hands, but the salt had hardened quickly since it had been disturbed. Grabbing his shovel, he dug at the earth in angry, furtive bites. He turned over a four-foot square pile of salt and dirt, but there was no gun or dog tags. Someone had been here before him, but who? The only person who even knew about the gun was his partner—and he was dead.

"You okay, buddy?"

Wayne jumped and then twisted around to see an older man standing over him.

"Uh . . . uh," Wayne stammered.

"I saw your car back there and stopped to see if you needed a lift back into town."

"Ah . . . no. My car works."

The older man's brows met in the center.

"Just overheated," Wayne said. "I'll be on my way shortly."

"Well, if you're sure. I saw that puddle under the back of your car and thought you might be in some trouble."

"Nope. The puddle was there when I stopped." Wayne could see that the man was inspecting the recently dug up pile before him. Wayne looked at the pile and then at the man. "I had to pee."

The man nodded and took a step back, turned and walked back toward the freeway.

Wayne stood up and after few moments followed him.

He let the man get in his truck and drive off before he approached his Taurus. As he did, he noticed the oil slick again.

This time he bent down and touched it. It was fresh. As he was rubbing the liquid goo off his fingers, his eyes caught the glimpse of something beneath the edge of his back wheel—a small piece of paper. He had to reach under his car to retrieve it. Frowning, he held up a limp, oil-soaked business card and read "Tip-of-the-Lake Towing."

Chapter 4

"Can you get a high lift under here?" Ben, Blake's friend, said to Lance as he looked at the white 4Runner, snuggly fit between Blake's Toyota truck and a dark blue Honda Accord in pieces.

"Should do," Lance said.

"Well, let's do it then," Ben said, walking toward the back of the barn to retrieve the jack.

Once lifted, they put blocks of lumber underneath four jack stands and proceeded to crawl under the rig with a flashlight.

"So what's your theory?" Ben asked.

"I think I lost a seal is all. I just put the tranny in, so that should still be fine. When I was on I-80, I noticed the gauges were going crazy, so I backed off and pulled over. I know I lost a lot of fluid, but by then I was coasting in, so I don't think I taxed it that much."

"Let's pull the pan anyway and see what you have, just

in case." Ben reached into a cherry red Snap-on toolbox and pulled out a Craftsman wrench and socket.

"Sure," Lance nodded.

After a few minutes of loosening bolts, they dropped the pan. They both looked at the contents in silence. Metal was everywhere: slivers, chunks, and nuggets—remnants of a badly thrashed transmission.

"Sorry, man," Ben finally said. "Is it under warranty?"

Lance shook his head to the negative; he was too frustrated to talk. Well, actually, there were quite a few words that were rattling around in his head at the moment, but none he felt like sharing with this Utah boy.

Finally Lance said, "I got the tranny from a wrecking yard in Rancho, near Sacramento. Anyway, it's cash and carry. It was so clean on the outside, I figured it would be fine. I paid almost $700 for it."

A low whistle escaped from between Ben's teeth. "What now?"

"I don't honestly know." Lance pulled himself out from under the truck, and Ben followed.

"Well, dude, there's nothing you can do tonight. Blake said you were spending the night. Do you want to watch a movie or play some video games?"

"Not really." Lance leaned back on the broken blue Honda.

"Do you have money for a new transmission?"

"Nope."

"What about your folks? Can you call them?"

Lance shook his head slowly, his lips sucked into his face.

"Oh," Ben said. "Understood."

"I can't believe this is happening. I'm going to have to get a job and find someplace to live, in Utah of all places, until I can fix it. Wait, how the heck am I going to get to a job if I don't have a car?" Lance let his head fall limply toward his chest.

"What?" Ben said. "You have a problem with Happy Valley?"

Lance let out a laugh-snort. "Well, I wasn't exactly planning on staying here, that's for sure. Too many Mormons—no offense, man."

"None taken. I couldn't agree more. As soon as I get enough in the bank, I'm out of here too," Ben said.

Lance lifted his head. "Really?"

"Yeah. I'm suffocating here, and it's not just small town blues. It's the whole culture. I don't fit in. I don't think I ever really have."

"But I thought you came from this big happy 'Mormony' family."

"Ah, looks can be deceiving."

"How old are you anyway?"

"Twenty-three. You?"

"Twenty-one," Lance said. "So you never went on a mission?"

"HE double toothpicks no."

Lance nodded. "Me neither. My folks wanted me to but there was just no way I could preach this whole happy family idea coming from such a messed up family myself."

"Actually, I may have misled you a bit. My family is not really messed up—it's more me. I think it's great for them. They couldn't be happier. I just think its mostly a bunch of . . ." His voice trailed off, and then he shook his head. "Anyway, why don't you plan on staying here with us until you figure this whole thing out. As for a job, I know a couple of places that are hiring if you don't mind working at night, and we'll figure out the transportation thing once you get hired."

"Thanks, man, and I actually prefer nights. Gives me more time to work on the Runner. So what's your sister's story?"

"Enin? Enin is just Enin. She's concerned for my 'eternal salvation,' so she makes up excuses to come out and cook for me and the guys. Hey, I'm no idiot. I'll take a home cooked meal over Micky D's any day."

"She seems a bit . . ." Lance started, but then he saw Ben's warning glance and said, "unusual is all."

"She's a good kid. She's smart, and to tell the truth, she's a better mechanic than I am."

"No way. She works on cars?"

"Yeah, that rig you saw her drive up in? She did everything but the welding. I suppose it helps that our dad owns a gas station in town. Enin intimidates most guys. You'd probably like her if you got to know her."

"The last thing I need in my life right now is a 'Mormon' chick. No thanks."

"Well anyway, you want to go to the Grub Box?"

"What the heck is a grub box?" Lance asked.

"Oh, I guess it's Magna's version of a Dairy Queen. It's a drive-thru, but mostly it's a hangout up on South Main."

"Uh, sure. You're driving though," Lance laughed.

"Well, actually I thought we'd invite Enin. Her truck is running better than mine right now."

"Hey, you're not trying to set me up with her are you?"

"No. I swear." Ben waved his hands. "It's about the trucks, really."

"All right."

Enin was sitting at the computer playing an early edition of Civilization when Lance and Ben walked in.

"You want to drive us to the Grub Box?" Ben said, motioning to Lance with his head.

"What's the matter with your truck?" she said, not taking her eyes from the screen.

"Among other things, my truck is almost out of gas."

"And my Runner's tranny is in pieces in the barn," Lance said.

Enin looked up from her game. "Really?"

"Yeah."

"That bad?"

"Worse," Ben added.

"So what now?" Enin said as she was saving the game.

"Get a job, I guess. Blake and your brother said I could stay here for a while."

Enin nodded and stood up. "Blake's nice like that." She winked at her brother and grabbed her lunch box. Lance stared at it.

"What? You don't like the *Dukes of Hazard?*" Enin said.

"No. No, I do. I love Daisy," he said. "But why the lunch box?"

"It's my lucky purse. Pretty much my whole life is in this thing. I'd be like one of those sorry BYU students without their Franklin day planners if I lost this purse."

The ride into town was more fun than Lance would have expected. Ben got in the front seat next to Enin, and he got in the back. When Enin headed out, she didn't go back down the driveway. She headed out behind the barn and through the fields. They went tumbling over the field, the Jeep responding to Enin's every command.

When they finally got to the highway, they settled into a quieter but fast ride toward town. Enin had put her Rhodes CD back in.

"Hey, you said you were from Sacramento, right?" Enin said.

"Rocklin actually," Lance answered.

"So how far is Rocklin from a place called Loomis?"

"Next to it."

"Really? This guy I'm listening to is from Loomis. Brian Rhodes. Do you know him?"

Lance shook his head.

Enin let her shoulders rise and fall.

Behind them they heard the annoying whine of a siren. Enin looked in her rearview mirror and sat up straighter. The boys turned around and saw the flashing lights bearing down on them.

"Oh, Enin's gonna get a ticket," Ben said in a singsong voice, clearly amused.

"Shut up," Enin said in return.

"Better not talk to the sheriff that way," Ben countered with a smile.

Lance sat quietly in the back, taking in the exchange between siblings.

Enin was not smiling as she pulled over on the side ledge of the road. With shaking fingers, she turned off the engine and waited for the officer to approach.

"Good evening, ma'am. Do you know why I stopped you tonight?"

"Uh, not really," Enin fibbed.

"Well, you were going 55 in a 35 mile per hour zone."

"Really?" Enin said feigning surprise.

"Really. Can I see your license? I'll need it out of your wallet."

"Sure," she said, reaching down to pull it out of her lunch box purse. With a crooked, awkward smile she handed it to the officer.

He walked back to his patrol car.

"Aren't you going to cry for the officer? I heard that helps sometimes," Ben said.

"Ben, really, just cool it," she said, the irritation in her voice rising.

The officer returned and handed her her licence and then a little clipboard with a pink ticket on it. "I'll need you to sign right here," he said, pointing to a line on the paper.

Enin looked at the ticket for a moment. The officer's name was Lanz; she had to appear in traffic court in July; and she'd been written up for going 45 in a 35 mile zone—well, that was good, she supposed.

"So can I do traffic school or something like that?" She paused, looked at the ticket, and then continued, "Sheriff Lanz?"

"That's up to the courts. But you can only do traffic court once every eighteen months."

"I've never done traffic school before," Enin said.

"Oh. Is this your first ticket?"

Enin nodded.

"Well, try to make it your last," Sheriff Lanz said coolly.

Enin nodded again as the officer turned and walked back to his car.

"Ooh, bummer about the ticket," Ben said, continuing to tease his sister.

Enin just folded the ticket and put it in her purse in response. She started the engine and slowly pulled back onto the road. The passengers were quiet the rest of the way into town.

When they pulled into the Grub Box, Ben said, "Hey look, Jared's here. That means Lance and I can catch a ride back with him."

"Good, 'cause I actually have to be at work early tomorrow," Enin said.

"Where do you work?" Lance asked, testing the waters with his benign question.

"At my dad's station."

"Mechanic?"

"No. Sales clerk—behind the counter."

"Hey, isn't that Mandy?" Enin looked at her brother warily.

All three looked in the direction of a very pregnant girl coming out the side door of the restaurant.

Lance saw Ben's jaw tighten. Ben's fist started to knead the soft covering of the roll bar he was holding. "Let's do the drive-thru," Ben said.

"I thought you might want to," Enin said as she pulled into the lane. Lance could hear the concern in her voice but hadn't known these two long enough to tell what signals they were sending each other.

"Actually, I've got to use the little boys room. Let me out here," Ben said. Without waiting for Enin to come to a full stop, he threw his legs over the side.

"Ben?" Enin said.

"I'm fine," he said, his back toward them both as he headed for the girl.

They watched him until a car honked behind them. They

had to move forward in the take-out lane.

"Old girlfriend," Enin said simply.

"I figured as much. Complicated?" Lance asked.

Enin looked straight into Lance's eyes, startling him with the penetrating blueness of them. "More than you will ever know, and no, the baby is not his. It's his best friend's."

Chapter

5

"Dad? Why do some people just get what the gospel is about and others. . . ." Her voice trailed off, and she continued to absently rearrange Life Savers in a box at the counter.

"Is this about Ben?" her dad asked.

"Isn't it always?" Enin wiped at an escaping tear.

"Well, honey, people have their free agency."

"This isn't about free agency, Dad. I know about free agency. Ben doesn't get it." Her voice was slightly rough. "Did he ever?"

"Have a testimony, you mean?"

"Yeah. Like when he was in Young Men's and stuff, did he have a testimony?"

Mosiah shrugged his shoulders. "He was never one to bear it in sacrament meeting, but he wasn't rebellious. Anyway, just because you stand up once or twice in testimony meeting doesn't mean you actually have one. There are lots of folks who just go through the motions."

"Sometimes I hate free agency," Enin said defiantly.

"Whoa, girl, you better be careful with that line of thought." Enin's dad reached across the counter and put his hand on her shoulder. "That's just what the adversary would like you to say."

"But I want Ben to be happy. I want him to understand what it's all about, but he won't listen to me. Sometimes I just want to shake him, or punch him, or throw water in his face so he'll come back to reality."

"This is his reality, Pumpkin, and right now he's not ready to listen to anyone."

"So what can I do? I feel so useless."

"Same as the rest of us—pray for him and then just love him, warts and all."

"But it seems like Heavenly Father isn't answering our prayers."

"Oh, he hears us all right, but Heavenly Father isn't going to force Ben either. That's the point."

"But it hurts, Daddy." Enin felt a little squeeze on her shoulder.

"I know, sweetheart, believe me, I know." Enin's dad turned to greet a customer coming in the store. "We'll talk later," he said, winking at his youngest daughter.

After work, as Enin was gassing up the Jeep, she saw Ben's Blazer drive down Main Street. Someone was in the passenger seat—probably that new kid, Lance.

She didn't think she liked Lance very much, especially since she'd heard from Blake that he was inactive as well. She didn't need anyone negatively influencing her brother. He was struggling enough on his own as it was.

When she pulled out, she saw them pulling out of Taco Time. They weren't that far ahead of her, so instead of turning toward home to do her geology report, she followed them.

They pulled into Billy's Big Parts Depot.

She pulled into Billy's behind them.

"Hey, guys!" she chirped, a little too forced.

"Enin, what're you doing here?" Ben said.

"Oh, I, uh, just left the station and thought I'd pop in and get a new set of spark plug wires."

Ben nodded.

"I thought you worked at a gas station. Can't you get that kind of stuff from your dad?" Lance asked, mildly suspicious.

Enin narrowed her eyes just a bit. "Of course I can, but I like Bosch, and Dad doesn't carry them."

"Oh," Lance said and shrugged his shoulders.

Does this kid think I'm stalking him, for heaven's sake? What an arrogant twit. She smiled Splenda sweet at Lance. "So what are you doing here?"

"I'm seeing about a job Ben heard about. I also need to price trannies."

"I wouldn't get your tranny from here!" Enin's eyes were wide with the shock of it. "They're the most expensive place in town."

"Not if I work here," Lance countered.

"Granted," she said. Not knowing what else to say, she turned back toward her Jeep.

"What about your spark plug wires?" Lance said.

She turned and her face became slightly red. "I, uh . . . I forgot my purse," she lied.

Lance smiled, his straight white teeth glistening in the sun. Then he nodded and winked.

Her eyes shot wide open in astonishment; she coughed once.

Lance turned and walked toward the parts house.

Enin didn't put the key in the ignition. She didn't adjust the mirrors. She didn't put on her seat belt. *Did that kid just wink at me? Like wink-wink? Like a guy winks at a girl? No way. Of all the people in the world to take an interest in me, does it have to be some egotistical, inactive kid from Cali?*

She closed her eyes and leaned her head on the headrest. *I'm exhausted. I had no business staying out so late when I had to be*

at work at five this morning. I need a nap. Well, first I need to get to
the library, but then a nap is definitely in order. My head is . . .

"You still here?" A voice interrupted her thoughts.

Enin jumped a little in her seat and opened her eyes. "What?"

"I said, 'Are you still here?'" Lance was casually leaning on her Jeep.

"I, uh, yes. I was just sitting here thinking."

"I see you found your purse." Lance looked directly at her lunch box sitting on the passenger seat.

"Oh," she laughed nervously. "Yeah. I, uh, thought I'd left it, but it was just on the floorboard."

"Well, I figured it couldn't have been far. After all, I knew you weren't like one of those 'silly BYU students who lose their Franklins,'" he grinned.

Enin grimaced that he could recall their previous conversation so accurately.

"Where's Ben?" she asked, looking over his shoulder toward the parts store.

"He's still looking around," he said, not taking his eyes off her.

"What about your interview?" Enin asked.

"No interview. I just came in to get this." He waved an application by his side. "I'm coming back Monday morning to meet with Joe something-or-other."

"Joe Travatillio," Erin said.

"Okay. That sounds right."

"He's a friend of my dad's."

"Makes sense," Lance said and then continued. "So what had you so wrapped up in thought?"

"You don't want to know."

"I might."

Enin looked him more closely. She thought she almost saw genuine concern in Lance's clear blue eyes.

"I'm worried about Ben."

Lance nodded and waited for her to go on.

"It's . . . well . . . I doubt if you are going to understand this, but my brother was pretty active in the Church before the whole thing with Mandy. Then he just gave up . . . and not just on the Church. He gave up on everything. His mission, his education, his family. It's been especially hard on my mom."

"Uh-huh."

"And . . . to tell the truth," she paused, but not for effect. She just wasn't sure she should go on but then did, rapidly. "I don't think your coming here is such a good thing for him."

Lance's head shot up and his brows furrowed.

"How did I get involved in your little family drama? I've been here, what, less than two days? You can't possibly blame me for your brother being inactive."

"No. I don't . . . but . . . well, it's just you're so much like him. I worry that the two of you . . ."

"What? That we'll go and get drunk? Does your brother drink?" Lance snapped.

"Well, no," Enin said.

"Neither do I. Does your brother smoke, or do drugs?" Lance pressed.

"Oh. Gosh no," Enin said, surprised anyone would ask that of a brother of hers.

"Well, neither do I. What evil plans do you think we're up to?"

Enin leaned her head forward and rested it on the steering wheel. "Okay. Maybe I'm overreacting," she said to the dashboard.

"Yeah, duh. You don't even know me, Enin," Lance said.

She shivered involuntarily at the sound of her name.

"I thought you left," Ben said to Enin over Lance's shoulder. This time, both Lance and Enin jumped slightly.

"Not yet," Enin smiled at Ben. "But I have to soon. I've got that stupid geology report due Monday, and the library closes at six."

"Why don't you get your stuff off the Internet?" Lance asked.

"I have to have one resource from the library—the real library—not the virtual kind."

Lance nodded.

"Does that mean you're not going to come to make us dinner tonight?" Ben asked.

"Sorry, boys, you're on your own," Erin replied.

"Well, that stinks," Ben said.

She spoke to Ben. "Are you going to go the dance tonight? I might be done in time for that."

"Dance? Since when do I go to the dances?"

"Oh, I don't know. I thought you might want to introduce Lance around."

"Nope," Ben said, shaking his head.

"What dance?" Lance asked.

"You wouldn't want to go," Ben said to Lance. "Just a bunch of stuck up Molly Mormons."

"Ben!" Enin said annoyed.

"Present company excluded," Ben smiled.

Enin let out a louder than usual sigh.

"Oh, don't go there, Enin. I was only kidding," Ben said sharply.

"Right. I believe that." Enin put her hand to the key and turned. The Jeep growled as it turned over. "Thing is Ben, you weren't. That's the problem." She put her hands on the steering wheel and started backing the Jeep out before Lance had time to step away. The side mirror brushed his temple.

"Whoa. She's got a temper too," Lance said, rubbing the side of his head.

"Uh, yeah," Ben said. "So what were you two talking about anyway?"

"You mostly."

Ben looked at Lance. "Me?"

"She thinks I'm out to corrupt you."

Ben huffed and shook his head. "She can be worse than my mom sometimes."

"What's the deal with that girl last night? Mandy."

"Enin told you about Mandy?" Ben's voice tightened.

"Not much. She said you used to date her and then she got pregnant by your best friend, well, I suppose your ex-best friend now."

"Ex is right. Did she tell you that Mandy broke up with me because I wouldn't go on a mission?"

"Nope."

"Did she tell you that Mandy married my best friend after he came home from his?"

"Nope. I didn't know she was married."

"It doesn't matter now. I'm over it." He pulled the door to his Blazer open a little too roughly and a loose piece of metal went flying.

"Oh yeah, I could tell," Lance said quietly to himself as he got in the other side.

Chapter

6

"Tip-of-the-Lake Towing. This is Amber. How may I help you?" The voice was sweet and high-pitched. Wayne smiled into the black receiver.

"I think I may have found some tools that belong to one of your drivers—Blake."

"Oh. Well, Blake won't be in until this evening," Amber said and then added, "Could I get your number and have him call you?"

"No!" Wayne said quickly. "I mean, no thanks. You see, I was going to be in the area, and I thought I could just drop them off—well, if they're his. I found them along westbound I-80 at mile marker 8."

"What makes you think they're Blake's?" Amber asked.

"Well, that's just it. I'm not sure if they even are. I found a set of ratchets in a case on the side of the road. I had stopped to fix a flat and Blake's business card was lying next to the tools in a pool of oil. I thought that maybe your driver might have left them when he was helping someone. But I suppose that would depend on if he was even out this way in the past couple of days."

"Oh, well that I can help you with. I'll just check the log book," Amber said helpfully.

Wayne sat on the side of his bed and bounced nervously as he heard Amber flipping through sheets of paper."

"Here it is, I think. It looks like Blake responded to a call late Thursday afternoon right at mile marker 8 on West bound I-80. Let's see, a 1990 white Toyota 4Runner—oh, wait, I remember that. That was the call from the young kid from California. It was weird, because normally Blake takes the vehicles to a shop or something, but he actually took this car to his own house in Magna. I think he was going to help the kid fix his truck or something. So I guess the tools might actually belong to the kid with the truck. Either way you'll want to talk to Blake directly," Amber finished.

"You've been very helpful, Amber. I'll call later tonight then," Wayne said, and he hung up the phone.

Wayne looked down at the Glock in his lap and spoke to it. "Well, that was easier than I thought it would be. How about you and me take a little side trip to Magna, Utah?"

Wayne stood up, pocketed his gun, and threw a faded green duffle bag over his shoulder. He had already paid up, and once this little matter in Utah was settled, he would be home free.

The trip to Magna took exactly ninety minutes. At 1:15 P.M. he was pulling off State Route 111 and headed toward the main part of town. He pulled into a Go-4-Gas on 2700 South. He put a little over twenty in his tank and walked into the air-conditioned mini-market. He was glad to see the attendant was a young white kid as opposed to either an older woman who tended to be nosey or a foreigner who seldom could give correct directions in English.

"Hi," Wayne said as he put down a cold Coke from the case and two one-dollar bills.

The clerk smiled back, took the money and rang up the beverage. He pushed a few coins back across the counter toward Wayne.

"Say, I don't suppose you know Blake Prescott?" Wayne asked. He wiped at a small frosting of sweat beading on his forehead.

"Sure. Went to school with him."

"I heard he lives around here still."

"Yeah. Him and Ben Woodson are renting the old Cooper place out on Tempo Road."

"Is that close to here?" Wayne asked, cautiously watching the kid's face closely.

"Yeah, not too far. It's up off of 8000 West."

Another customer walked in, and the young man's attention was diverted; Wayne slipped a local map into his pocket and left the store.

Not only was Tempo Road close, but the Coopers had graciously left their name on the rusting roadside mailbox. If everything went as smoothly as it had today, he would be back on the road in twenty-four hours.

He didn't want to spend the money on another hotel, so he spread the newly acquired map on the faded gray velour seat of his car. He found a campground not too far from Magna. It would do.

When he got to the spot on the map, a small handwritten sign on the highway said it was closed for renovations and not to enter. The official sign behind it was pockmarked with bullet holes. He ignored the warning and drove down the deserted dirt road. It snaked back toward the scrubby hills and ended at a small grove of trees with ten or twelve campsites and an outhouse. For him it was perfect; he just needed a place to hang out until dark. He got in the backseat of his car, stretched out, and promptly fell asleep.

Chapter 7

Lance heard the high-pitched, rhythmic chirping of birds outside and opened one eye and then the other. Because he hadn't put in his contacts yet, he soft-focused on the blue of an unfamiliar wall. A framed picture of Christ hung next to an open window, white curtains billowing slightly in the dry, early morning breeze. He closed his eyes again and rubbed them while yawning.

Opening them a second time, the scene had not changed, but he was having trouble in his almost-but-not-quite-awake-yet-state figuring out what he was seeing. He knew he didn't have blue walls in his bedroom, and his friends would have pictures of punk rock bands on their walls, so where the heck was he?

He rolled over and looked up. He was in the bottom of a bunk bed, the bunk bed just then groaning slightly under the weight of someone turning over above him. Blake. Blake was above him, and this was Blake's bedroom. Blake was the kid he was staying with. Slowly Lance was waking up. He rub-scratched his head with both hands. He was in Utah, and his 4Runner was in pieces in the garage—no, barn—out back.

He looked at his watch: five after nine. Wow, that was early for him, but he knew once awake, he wouldn't be going back to sleep. He threw his feet over the bed and ducked his head to miss the upper boards of the bed. He padded to the bathroom in his boxers—it was, as he recalled, an all-boy's establishment.

"You're up early."

Lance turned toward the voice behind him. He yawned and nodded.

"Are you up for the day?" Ben said.

"Once up," Lance nodded and yawned one more time, "no matter how tired I am, I'm up."

"How late were you up last night anyway?"

"I don't know, 'til three o'clock or so. We were working on that Honda." Lance put his hand over his mouth to stifle yet another yawn.

"Oh."

"I didn't see you last night. Did you end up going to that dance with your sister?" Lance asked.

"Oh, heck no!" Ben laughed and continued. "I was out shooting with some friends. There's this place outside of town we go to. Usually the cops leave us alone, and we set up targets and stuff."

"What do you shoot?"

"Oh, I just use the other guy's stuff. He's got a personal arsenal, nothing illegal of course, but he has a shotgun, a Glock, a Beretta, and a little twenty-two."

"Wait here." Lance went back in his bedroom and pulled the gun he had found from under his mattress.

He walked into the hallway with the gun. He handed it to Ben. "It's not loaded."

Ben took it carefully and turned it side to side. "Yours?"

"It is now. I found it alongside the road when I broke down."

"Just lying on the road?" Ben asked, his eyebrows meeting in the center.

"Well, not on the asphalt, but not too far from it."

Ben nodded as he looked more closely at it. "Does it have the clip?"

"Yeah, but it was a little stuck, so I think the gun needs cleaning," Lance said.

"My buddy could probably do it for you. Maybe we'll catch up with him later today. Hey, you want to work on your truck this morning?"

"Yeah, but I'm not too sure what I can do without money."

"Well, we could drop the tranny, clean up the oil—that kind of thing," Ben said.

"Sure. I was gonna take a shower to wake up, but I'll wait then. I do have to put my contacts in though."

"Good enough. I'm eating first. There's some cereal above the fridge, or if you're into cooking, you can make eggs."

"Cereal's fine."

Ben turned back toward the kitchen, and Lance entered the bathroom.

Face washed, teeth brushed, and contacts in made a big difference in how Lance saw the day. Whistling, he pulled a box of Frosted Flakes off the top of the old Kenmore. Clean, mismatched bowls and silverware were on a towel next to the sink.

"So I was thinking if we took the tranny apart, maybe we could get the stuff to fix it ourselves," Lance said.

"You ever rebuilt one before?" Ben said, draining the last gulp of his OJ out of his plastic tumbler.

"No, but I've never been this broke before either."

"Well, I suppose it couldn't hurt to take it apart and look at it. My dad's done it before, but he says it's such a chore that he usually sends his out to be rebuilt. If you end up getting a new one, I suppose they'll still take the old one in pieces for the core charge."

"Yeah, that's what I was thinking. Basically, what do I have to lose?" Lance said.

"True that."

"I thought these guys went to church on Sunday," Lance said, nodding his head toward the closed bedroom doors.

"They do. They go to the singles ward. It doesn't start 'til two."

"And you?"

"I don't go anymore, singles or otherwise."

Lance nodded, got up, rinsed his bowl, and put it in the sink.

Ben did the same. Leaving the house, they headed for the barn.

"Idiots!" Ben said as he pulled open the wide barn doors.

Lance stopped. He could see tools strung all over the place.

"What did you guys do last night?" Ben looked at Lance, his words clipped.

Lance continued staring wordlessly.

"Well?" Ben said, his voice getting hot with anger.

"Ah, I don't know what's going on. We . . ." He walked into the barn and looked at the mess surrounding the cars. His 4Runner doors were open, the tailgate was down. The gray and black neoprene seat cover that usually covered the rips in the torn vinyl was thrown carelessly on the dirt floor. The Honda was intact, but the tools they had left in the box next to it were dumped all over the barn. The doors on Blake's 'Yota were open, and the seat had been removed and was out of his truck. Someone had rifled through it also.

"Whoa, man," Ben said as he looked around the barn more carefully. "What's going on?"

"I don't know." Lance turned to face Ben. "It's your barn. I thought Utah was supposed to be above this kind of stuff."

"Looks like someone tried to steal either your rig, or Blake's."

"Why would someone try to steal my truck? Anyone with brains can see the dropped oil pan underneath it."

"Vandals maybe?" Ben corrected.

"Maybe." Lance's voice slowed in thought. "But they didn't really damage my truck," he said as he walked around it. "Other than pulling off the seat covers, my truck looks okay. Although they did go through my stuff. My tent is out of its bag. What about the Honda?"

"It looks okay," Ben said as he walked around it. "Should we call the police?"

"I don't know. What do you usually do in a case like this?"

Ben shrugged. "Never really had a case like this before. Is any of your stuff missing?"

"Not that I can tell," Lance said as he stooped down to pick up the seat covers.

"I suppose we should get Blake and Jared out here. But you're right, there's no way they did this."

"No. It was just Blake and me anyway. Jared was in bed. Blake and I went to bed around three, like I said. This had to have happened after that," Lance said.

"Well, shoot. I'll go get them up, I guess."

"Okay, I'll start picking up stuff. Looks like it was probably just some punk kids looking for trouble." Lance ran a hand over his 4Runner, his fingers leaving a four-lane trail in the salty, dirty dust.

Blake and Jared were either angrier than Ben and Lance or just annoyed that they had been woken up early. Lance didn't know either of them well enough to tell the difference. After a frustrating half hour, the garage and cars were sort of back to normal. Blake thought they should call the sheriff's department, but Jared thought it would be a waste of "taxpayers' money," and besides, it was Sunday. Jared figured they should leave the sheriff alone if they could. They decided that if Blake really wanted to tell someone about the break-in, he could just tell Deputy Butler, who was also Bishop Butler of the Magna

Stake Singles Ward, at church later that day.

By 1:30 P.M., Jared and Blake were backing out of the driveway for church, and Ben and Lance were covered in transmission oil and grease.

"You want to go into town and get something to eat?" Ben asked as he wiped the oil off a wrench he was putting away.

"Don't they roll up the sidewalks here on Sunday?" Lance asked honestly.

"A lot of places do, but not the McDonald's near the freeway."

"Then sure, but can I clean up first? I need a quick shower."

Ben looked down at himself and nodded. "Me too. Why don't you go now?"

"Are you sure? I mean I hate to leave you with the clean-up."

"Not that much left to do now. We already cataloged what parts we're going to need, and I'm just going to wipe down these tools and put them away. That should give you enough time to get cleaned up."

Lance hesitated, "Well, okay. I won't be long."

The phone was ringing as Lance entered the kitchen. He looked toward the barn and then picked the receiver up.

"Ah," he hesitated for a moment. *Whose residence was this anyway?* "Hello?" he finally said.

A soft laugh came from the handset. "Hello, Lance."

He recognized Enin's voice and sighed. "I know, that sounded lame. I was going to say 'Raintree residence,' which is how I answered the phone at home, but obviously I wasn't home. Then I realized I didn't know Blake's last name, so I couldn't answer it that way either."

"For future reference, Blake's last name is Prescott, and I didn't know your last name was Raintree."

"It's not. Raintree is my stepmother's new husband."

"Uh?"

Lance shook his head as if Enin could see. "Don't worry about it. It's too complicated."

"Just one more question, okay?" Enin said.

"Shoot."

"Do you have a middle name?"

"No," Lance said with hesitation, lying into the phone.

"Really?" Enin had picked up on his slight pause.

"Really," Lance said sharply.

"Oh . . . ah . . ." The line went silent.

"I suppose you called for Ben," Lance said.

"Yeah, I did," Enin responded with a chill in her voice.

"He'll be in in a minute. He's shutting the doors now. We pulled the tranny apart. Do you want to wait or call back?"

"Wait."

"That's fine," Lance fibbed, a little frustrated that he wasn't in the shower yet.

"So," Enin said, "why'd you pull the transmission apart. You're not planning on rebuilding it yourself, are you?"

"Well, yeah, I was," Lance said, slightly offended.

"Ooh, that's a big job."

"I know that, but if you'll recall, I have no job and no money. What else am I going to do?" Lance's voice was a little more prickly than he intended.

"Uh . . . I guess I see your point. I could help if you like."

"Help? How? You ever rebuilt a transmission?"

"Yes, in school," Enin said simply.

"Figures," Lance whispered too low for Enin to hear, as Ben walked through the door. "Oh, hey, here's Ben. Talk at you later. Bye." Lance handed the phone to Ben without explanation and walked toward the bathroom.

Chapter

8

"Hello?" Ben said into the phone.

"Hi," Enin said to her brother.

"Oh. It's you. Lance just handed me the phone."

"I figured as much. He's weird."

"Not at all," Ben said. "He's actually a pretty nice guy."

"I don't know. Every time I talk to him he's weird with me. He's sort of . . ." Enin had to stop and think before she went on. "Well, it's like he has some secret family thing going on, and he gets mad at you if you bring it up, but you didn't know you were bringing it up in the first place."

"What?" Ben said.

"He's just mixed up or—" She was cut off midsentence.

"Never mind about him, what'd you call for?"

"Oh, I was going to ask if you wanted dinner tonight, but—"

Ben cut her off again.

"We're going to McDonald's in a minute, and Blake and Jared won't be back 'til after eight. They have some singles ward thing."

"Ben!" Enin said, exasperated.

"What?" Ben said.

"That's the second time you cut me off."

"Oh, sorry. That stupid break-in has me rattled, I guess."

"What break-in?" Enin said, her voice rising a bit.

"Oh. I guess you wouldn't know. Some punk kids broke in the garage last night. They threw things around, pulled stuff out of the trucks and that old Honda we've been working on. Mostly just made a mess, but it was weird, you know?"

"Did you call the sheriff?" Enin said.

"Nah. Nothing was missing. We decided not to bother him on Sunday. I suppose Blake might mention it to Bishop Butler today at church, but I don't really expect anyone to come out. It's not that big of a deal."

"How about the tools? Any of them missing?"

"No. Nothing was missing that we could tell. Blake, Jared, and I all checked."

"Do you think Lance had anything to do with it?" Enin said.

"Lance? Oh, heck no. Now you're just being paranoid. Lance was out working on the Honda with Blake until about three. Jared was in bed. I was out shooting. No one heard a thing."

"How about tire tracks? Maybe it was someone you go wheeling with."

"Listen Detective Enin, just leave the mystery to us. I'm sure it was just some local kids messing around. Nothing was damaged. No harm done."

"Well, I have to come over anyway. I left one of my books there the other day. It's next to the computer."

"Some science book?" Ben asked.

"Yeah, geology."

"Well, it'll be here, but we may not. After lunch we may

go out shooting," Ben said.

"No problem. I can let myself in." Enin hesitated for just a moment before she continued. "Mom wants to know if you need anything?"

"No. Tell her I'm fine. I'll try and come by tomorrow."

"Tomorrow's her birthday," Enin said, mildly surprised that Ben was coming over.

"Duh. I know that. Why do you think I just said I'd come over?"

"She'll be happy to hear from you is all."

"Enin, I'm not the spawn of Satan. I know it's Mom's birthday. Don't make such a big deal out of this. I even got her a present. How's that?"

"That's great. Really great," Enin said in a quiet, metered voice.

"Enin, don't do that."

"Do what?" Enin said.

"Get all weird on me. You get that tone of voice like Mom. It bugs the heck out of me."

"I . . ."

"All right. I gotta go and take a shower. Maybe I'll see you later, and if not tonight, then tomorrow for sure."

Enin stood with the receiver in her hand, head down, thinking. After a few seconds, the busy tone startled her into putting it back in its cradle. Her father walked into the family room.

"What's up, Pumpkin? You look like you got some bad news."

"Oh, do I?" Enin lifted her eyes to look at her father. A good-looking man, he had broad shoulders and an almost flat stomach, unlike many other fathers in the ward. It was like looking at Ben thirty years down the road. "No. I actually got good news. That was Ben. He's coming over to see Mom tomorrow for her birthday."

Her dad nodded. "Good. That'll be a nice present for her. What are your plans for this afternoon?"

"Oh, I have to run over to Ben's and pick up a book I left so I can finish my homework, and then I have to go visiting teaching with Becky Costello."

"So when do you expect to be home?"

"I don't know, maybe five or so. I may go back to Ben's and read. It's a little quieter over there."

They both turned toward a large crashing sound in the kitchen.

"It's cool," they heard her younger brother yell from the kitchen.

Her dad sighed and then laughed. "Understood. Maybe I should come over there with you to get my home teaching routes mapped out."

"Maybe you should. No one's home right now," Enin said.

"Nah, I'll stay here. You go and get some reading done." Her dad turned and walked into the kitchen.

Enin was halfway to Ben's house when she realized she'd left her phone on the charger. She almost turned around but decided that she could live a few hours without it and kept driving. If she needed to call anyone, Ben had a phone at his place.

Turning down the gravel driveway, she noticed a gray Taurus with California plates parked by the barn.

Chapter

9

Wayne watched the Jeep bumping down the gravel driveway. He looked at his watch. He'd only been here fifteen minutes, and hopefully he'd only be here another few. Tapping his foot rapidly on the wooden front porch, he thought about California and the beach he remembered from Camp Pendleton. The cheap plastic lawn chair he was sitting on wiggled unsteadily as he tap-tap-tapped away.

A young girl got out of the Jeep and smiled tentatively as she got closer.

"Hi. Can I help you?"

"I hope so," said Wayne. "I'm looking for Blake Prescott."

"Well, this is the right place, but he's not here right now," the girl said.

"When do you think he'll be back?" Wayne noticed her small, hesitant movements as she ascended the wooden steps.

She paused at the top of them and set down what looked like a small child's lunch pail.

"Oh," the girl said. "It's hard to tell. He might be here any minute, or he could be another couple of hours. He's at church. Is there something I can help you with?"

"Well, maybe. I talked to Amber down at the tow yard, and she said Blake might have something of mine that got left in my car when he towed it the other day. I thought I'd come over and ask him if he's seen it before I file a report with my insurance."

"Amber?" was all the girl said. She backed down one step.

Wayne stood up. "Maybe you could just help me look around."

The girl stepped back one more time and caught her heel on the edge of the step. She started to teeter. Wayne took a quick step closer and grabbed her arm.

"Why don't we go inside and maybe you could help me look for it?" Wayne said. The girl tried to pull her arm free, but Wayne tightened his grip on it. "Be a good girl, and no one is going to get hurt. I just need to find my stuff, and I'll be on my way."

"I don't know where your stuff is. I'm no help to you. I have to go." She was struggling to break free.

"I'm not kidding around here, uh, what's your name?"

"Brittany," she said after a moment's hesitation. He thought she might be lying.

"I'm not kidding around here, *Brittany*. I only need what belongs to me, and then I'll leave. The sooner you help me find it, the sooner I can get out of here. Do you understand?"

He pulled the Glock out of his pocket with his free hand and waved it in the girl's face. "Do you understand?"

The girl paled and went still. She nodded.

"Do you have a key?" Wayne asked.

"No. The back door's not locked," she said.

Wayne pulled her down the steps and onto the gravel. He

walked her toward the back of the house. She was not resisting. That was good. Glocks had that effect on people.

"What are you looking for?"

"A gun. A Beretta to be exact. It's part of a valuable gun collection."

"I don't remember Blake saying anything about a gun."

"Where is his room?" Wayne said as they entered the kitchen.

"Down the hall; it's the blue one."

"Sit here," Wayne motioned with his head to one of the wooden chairs next to the table, "and don't try anything funny. I've already cut the phone lines. If you do try to leave, I'll hear you, and I can guarantee a bullet from this gun is faster than you are." Wayne waved the Glock in her face. "Better yet," he continued, setting the gun on the table and reaching into a different pocket. He pulled out a roll of silver duct tape. The girl's eyes widened. He pulled one arm behind her and reached for the other.

"I'm not going anywhere. You don't have to do this," the girl said. Her voice trembled slightly as he pulled her other arm tightly behind her back.

"Experience tells me I do," Wayne replied. He proceeded to duct tape her wrists together.

"Ow," she said.

"The less you move, the less it hurts," Wayne offered. He then pulled a red bandana out of his shirt pocket. He held it and the duct tape up. "Your choice," he said, smiling.

"Ah. . ." the girl said.

"I'll give you a hint. You can breathe easier with the bandana around your mouth."

The girl's head dropped onto her chest.

"Bandana it will be then." Wayne put the red cloth around her face and head, forcing her mouth open, and then tightening the knot in the back. "Now you just sit here while I go look for my stuff."

Wayne went into the bedroom. Pulling things out of

dresser drawers and off closet shelves didn't take long. He lifted the mattresses on the upper bunk bed and then the lower bunk. He froze when he saw a thin silver chain on the lower bunkie board. The bunkie board was only two inches thick with a rip in the top of the fabric. The chain disappeared into the tear in the mattress support. He was close. He pulled on the chain, and the dog tags came out. He reached his hands into the hole and tore at it, looking for his gun. Not finding it between the first set of support struts, he tore the fabric further until nothing was left but ribbons of fabric on a wooden frame. He swore.

After a few minutes, he came out of the bedroom, sweat lighting on his forehead. Large wet rings were creeping down his black T-shirt. He had the dog tags in one hand, dangling from a chain.

Looking at the girl, he said. "Well, he's got it all right, but it's not in his bedroom."

"Mm b, iss inn."

"Hold on." Wayne reached around the girl and untied the bandana.

The girl opened her mouth wide to stretch it.

"What?"

"Maybe it's in his work truck," she volunteered.

Wayne nodded. "Good point. Why don't we go see?"

She shook her head slowly. "No thanks. You go without me."

"Funny. Very funny. No, I think you're coming with me." Wayne grabbed her arm and pulled her up, knocking the chair over. "Here's the deal. You scream, and I'll use the duct tape *and* put you in the trunk. Do you understand?"

She nodded.

As they started toward the Taurus, a car drove by on Tempo Road. Wayne waited until the sedan had rounded the bend before he shoved the girl forward. He opened the passenger side door and pushed her in.

"Can I have my hands in front? This hurts," the girl said.

"No. Deal with it," Wayne said as he shut the door.

Getting in the driver's side, he started the car. He made a three-point turn and headed out the driveway. Getting on Tempo, he headed north and then west on 8000. He noticed the girl tense up and turn her head quickly when they passed a slow moving truck at the intersection of 8000 West. She probably knew the old geezer—that wouldn't do. He snaked over to Route 111 and headed west again.

"Blake's work is the other way," she said.

Wayne detected a little quiver in her voice and smiled. "I know," he said as he continued to drive toward the foothills.

"Where are we going then?" she asked.

"Camping," Wayne smiled.

Chapter 10

"So do you want to go see my buddy, or go back to the house?" Ben said as he pulled his Blazer out of McDonald's.

"Let's go see your buddy. I'm going a little stir crazy right now."

"Gotcha." Ben waited at the signal on 8000 West and watched a gray Taurus cut off some old man. "What a jerk."

"Yeah. That looked like Enin in the car," Lance observed.

"What? The Taurus? I didn't notice," Ben said.

"Yeah. Aah . . . all Mormon chicks probably look alike."

"Yeah," Ben agreed. "Mine did. That whole long-hair-in-a-ponytail thing. Sweetly deceiving smile." He turned and flashed a toothy smile at Lance.

"Do I detect a note of bitterness?"

"Duh? She turned out to be such a jerk. I can't believe I wasted so many good years on her."

"How long did you date her?" Lance asked.

"Six years."

"Six years! That's a long time."

"I know. My point exactly," Ben said.

"When did you meet?"

"The summer we both turned fourteen."

"But you didn't start dating then, did you? I mean Mormon chicks don't date until they're sixteen," Lance said.

"Well, technically, we didn't date. We met at stake dances and stuff like that. Our parents knew we were 'seeing each other,' but they preferred to just ignore it. It was pretty okay. Everybody just assumed we would be getting married after my mission. Heck, even I thought that."

"But then you didn't go," Lance said.

"Right. Well, at first I was just toying with not going, but it freaked Mandy out so much that it bothered me. I mean, why was my going on a mission such a big deal to her? The more I thought about it, the more angry I got. Next, she would be pressuring me to become a bishop and then a stake president. I was beginning to see what she really wanted from me, and I just didn't think I could deliver. I can tell you right now, I'm not general authority material."

Ben turned toward his friend's house.

"So she broke up with you?"

"No, I broke up with her. It was the best and worst thing I ever did. Then my best friend left on his mission. No big deal. He went to Uruguay. I didn't know he and Mandy wrote the whole time. She told me later they would mostly discuss me and how they could get me to go on my mission." Ben paused so he could concentrate on making a left. "Anyway, I guess one thing led to another, and when he got home, he married her."

"Is that when you left your folks' house?"

"No, I left about a year before that. My mom was always moping around the house. I knew it was because I was still home and not on a mission. I just got tired of the drama."

"So that's the end of that chapter of your life."

"Well, almost. The only thing I still need to do is get back all the letters and stuff I wrote to Mandy, so I can have a heck of a big bonfire. I keep asking her for the stuff, but she's real evasive. She says the stuff is in the bedroom closet at her old house."

"So why don't you go there and get it?"

Ben tapped his fingers on the steering wheel. "You know, Lance, you're right. Why don't I?" With that said, Ben yanked hard on the steering wheel and flipped a U-ee. "Let's go now."

"Now?"

"Sure, why not? She doesn't live there anymore, and I happen to know her parents are out of town."

"How will we get in?" Lance asked practically.

Laughing, Ben responded. "No one locks doors around here, or didn't you notice?"

Ben broke a few speed limits on his way back to Magna. Once there he made a few lefts and rights and pulled up in front of a pale gray and white split-level brick home.

Ben hopped out of the truck. "Come on," he said to Lance.

Lance shrugged his shoulders and got out. He followed Ben down a set of basement stairs under the carport.

Ben opened the door at the bottom of the stairs and gave Lance an "I told you so" look.

Lance followed Ben inside. The room was dark, except for the light that was coming in the two high-set windows that faced the front of the house.

Ben stopped for a moment and took a deep breath.

"Funny. It still smells the same," Ben said.

Lance took in a deep breath too. It smelled dusty and sort of old to him. He coughed.

"Come on, her room's down here."

He opened a door and stopped so suddenly that Lance walked into him.

"Is that you, boys?" A tiny voice came from the hospital

bed set under the high window. "I've been expecting you."

"Uh," Ben stammered.

"Come in, come in. I've been waiting all afternoon."

Lance looked at Ben.

"She's blind," Ben whispered to Lance.

"Of course I'm blind. You don't have to be afraid, boys. Just come in and set up next to the bed here."

"Set up?" Lance said, confused.

"The sacrament. You boys came over to administer the sacrament, right?"

"Well, no, not exactly," Ben said.

"Is that you, Ben?" the tiny voice said excitedly.

"Yes, Grandma, it's me."

"The bishop sent you over? That's wonderful. Just wonderful."

"Well, no, Grandma, I didn't really come for that. I came to get some stuff out of Mandy's closet."

"Oh." Her voice fell, disappointment apparent to Lance. "Who's that with you?" she said.

"Oh, sorry, Grandma. This is my friend Lance."

"Uh, hi," Lance said uncomfortably.

"Lance, this is Mandy's great-grandmother. Apparently, she lives here now. She used to live a few blocks over."

"Nice to meet you, Lance, and that's right, I did live a few blocks from here. Ben and Mandy used to sneak over and smooch in my back bushes when they thought I wasn't looking."

Ben's face reddened.

Lance laughed nervously.

"So did you ever go on your mission?"

"Uh, no," Ben said.

"Benjamin Woodson! What *is* the matter with you, boy?"

"Grandma, missions aren't for everyone," he pleaded.

"Not for everyone? We aren't talking about everyone here. We're talking about you. You give me one good reason why you aren't on a mission right now!"

"Well," Ben started.

"And don't you use that old excuse about Mandy marrying your best friend. You and Mandy were never meant to be in the first place."

"Grandma," Ben said.

"Well? I'm still waiting."

"Okay, for one I don't believe in the Church anymore," Ben said.

"Balderdash. I don't believe that for a minute. I know you, Ben Woodson. How many times did you read the Book of Mormon in high school?"

"That's not fair," Ben protested.

"How many?" Grandma insisted.

"Six, but that's not the point. Anyone could have read the Book of Mormon that many times. It doesn't mean the Church is true."

"Stop! Now you stop that right now, Ben. Look me in the eyes and tell me you don't believe the book is true—and don't you mind that I'm blind. I can tell if you're looking at me or not."

Ben lowered his head.

"Ben?" Grandma insisted.

"I can't," Ben said, and Lance was surprised to see what might pass for tears in his new friend's eyes. If he wasn't careful, Lance might start crying himself, though he didn't know why.

"That's what I thought. Ben, you are prideful! You know that? Prideful. The Lord hates prideful men. What makes you think you're above the rest of us? Sure you got hurt, but no one intended that. There's someone else out there for you. Mandy wasn't the one, that's all. Now you leave her be, you hear me, you leave her be. Get over your silly pining for her. She's not going to take the blame for you not going on your mission, you know that, don't you? It's all about you, Ben."

"I know, Grandma," Ben said, his voice cracked from the constriction in his throat.

"Now, you just go home and talk this whole thing out with your bishop, you hear?"

"Yes, Grandma," Ben said softly.

"You promise me, Ben?"

"I promise," Ben said.

"And next time you come I want it to be with you bringing me the sacrament."

Ben nodded silently.

Even though Lance knew Grandma couldn't see the action, he felt certain this old woman knew all the same, because she nodded back and smiled.

Chapter 11

Enin was grateful this horrid man hadn't blindfolded her. She had had a silent prayer in her heart since the minute she had set eyes on his car. She wouldn't talk now, but as they rolled down the highway, she paid attention to every detail around her.

As near as she could figure, this man was about five foot ten. He had a paunch around the middle that he tried to hide by wearing baggy clothes. He had on a pair of dirty camouflage cargo pants and what looked like army boots covered in white dust, or possibly salt.

She knew she was being kidnapped, and she was scared— but at the same time, she had a strange calmness surrounding her. This guy wanted his gun back, but he didn't strike her as a pervert—just a sad, crazy man.

She knew she wasn't going to be missed for a while. No one expected her home for hours. By the time Jared and Blake got back from church, it would be almost dark. She didn't know when Ben and Lance would get back. And how weird was that—that she saw Ben and Lance waiting at a light as they passed that old man in the truck. She wished with all her heart that Ben had seen her, but his head was turned the other way.

The scenery out her window was familiar. She had grown up in Magna and had been in these hills hundreds of times. She knew right where she was, but she was counting on her "host" not to. She was fairly certain he was not from around here, and not just because he had California license plates. It was more because of the map he kept glancing at in his lap.

They were coming up to a particularly familiar sight, the place where Ben and his friends went shooting. She was slightly startled when her "host" turned right onto the dirt road. He took the deserted road to the camping area and didn't even seem to notice the other, better-traveled road to the north of it.

He pulled into site #3, turned off the car, and sat for a minute. He hadn't said one word to her on the way to the campground, and she was hoping he would keep up the silence. His voice creeped her out.

"Do you have a cell phone?" he said.

"Not with me," Enin said.

He nodded. He pulled out his map and looked at it again. After a few minutes, he folded it up as close as he could to the original.

"I've got to go back to town and take care of some things. You'll need to stay here."

"Here where?" Enin blurted out as she looked around the desolate campground.

"The outhouse."

Enin would have said 'You're kidding,' but she knew he wasn't, so she didn't say anything more; she was praying silently.

The awful man got out of the car and came around to her side. The door made a creaking, popping sound as it opened. Enin recognized it as a badly aligned door; the car had probably been in an accident and poorly fixed.

He touched her elbow in an effort to help her up, but she pulled it in tight to the side of her waist, even though doing so caused her to wince. Scooting her bottom over and balancing herself, she stepped out of the car. She would go to the stupid outhouse and figure it out from there. She was scared but not hysterical—at least not yet.

She walked in front to the outhouse. The man opened the door. A hundred flies came buzzing out, but a few stayed behind. Shuddering and taking a deep breath, she started coughing from the stench.

"Can you at least put the lid down?" Enin said sharply.

"Uh, yeah," the man said, reaching in and closing the lid—though the smell remained as strong as ever.

"May I have my hands in front this time?" Enin asked very politely.

"I'd prefer not," the man said.

Enin lowered her head like a two year old but kept her eyes on the man from under her long dark lashes. She sniffed once.

The man just stood there.

"Oh, all right," the man finally said, "but I'm still going to have to put that thing in your mouth and tape your feet, so don't think you're going anywhere soon."

Enin nodded. With her hands in front, a lot of possibilities would open up for her.

"You're going to have to step through your arms."

Enin squinched her face in puzzlement.

"Come on, Brittany, you never seen *Cops*? You slide down and pull your legs through one at a time."

Enin thought, *Why doesn't that surprise me that this guy's a* Cops *fan?*

She sat on the stoop of the outhouse and wiggled her bottom under her hands first and then one leg at a time, just like he said. She was mildly astonished that it worked the first time.

"Okay, go on. Get in there; I'm in a hurry. The sooner I

get my gun back, the sooner I leave, understand?"

Rolling over and balancing herself on her forearms, she stood up. She stepped into the wooden structure.

Removing a flattened roll of duct tape out of his pocket, he said, "Put your legs together."

She did. He banded them tightly and took her shoes off, setting them neatly outside the door. Pulling the red bandana out of his pocket, he waved it in front of her face.

"Bend over," he said.

She knew he meant her head, so she complied. He gagged her again. This time the taste and smell of the old bandana made her stomach churn.

The man backed out the door and shut it. She could hear the sound of duct tape pulling away from itself. He kicked dust up as he rounded the outhouse; little puffs came though the old, cracked boards. He rounded the cubicle at least twice, which meant there were two, or possibly more, bands of duct tape between her and freedom.

His footsteps got fainter; then she heard car doors being shut. Silence—he was probably studying his map again. The engine started, sputtered, and backfired. She held her breath. "Oh, please, Heavenly Father, let the car start," Enin whispered. On the second try, the Taurus started up. The sound of tires got fainter and fainter until it disappeared altogether.

Enin used her relatively free hands to loosen and then pull the gag from her mouth. It was a start.

Chapter 12

Ben hadn't said a word since they left Mandy's old house. Lance respected his silence. They drove away from town, which mildly surprised Lance. Lance thought that given the tone of the conversation with the old woman that Ben would head straight to a bishop's house, any bishop's house.

"You thirsty?" Ben said, startling Lance.

"Ah, yeah. Sort of."

"I'm gonna stop at a Mini Mart and get a pop."

"Pop?" Lance said, puzzled.

Ben laughed. "Right, you're not from around here. You call them sodas. In Utah, they're pop."

"Why pop?"

"I don't know, they just are. There aren't many places to stop around here even if it wasn't Sunday. I just thought you might be thirsty again, or even hungry after only eating one cheeseburger."

"Yeah," Lance laughed, "I'm a little of both actually."

"Well, you can get a hot dog or deli sandwich here," Ben said as he pulled into the convenience market and parked.

Lance walked toward the front door, but Ben veered off toward the right. He headed for the restrooms on the side of the old converted gas station.

A blast of cool air hit Lance in the face. At the counter, a slightly overweight girl stood watching him as he went to the soda case. He grabbed a large bottle of Mountain Dew and walked over to the hot food case. Biting his lower lip, he considered the greasy chicken, soggy sandwiches, and slightly dull looking hot dogs, and then he backed away. He went to the snack aisle instead. A bag of cashews, Snickers, Baby Ruth, and M&M's would hold him over while he was out shooting.

Lance turned toward the sound of the opening doors.

"So did you get something to eat?" Ben asked.

"Yeah, it's cool. I'm good," Lance said, watching the plump girl watch him.

Ben went to the soda case and grabbed an orange soda.

When he returned, he said, "I called my friend. He said to meet him out at the range in fifteen."

"Okay. So the range is close?"

"Yeah, it's not really a range. It's an old quarry outside of town."

Ben set his stuff next to Lance's. He handed the girl a twenty. Lance reached into his pocket, and Ben said, "I'll get it this time. When you're gainfully employed, you can return the favor."

"Thanks," Lance said, and he put the snack food in his pocket. They walked back to the car and got in.

Easing onto the highway, Ben said. "Sorry you had to be pulled into that mess back at Mandy's house."

Lance nodded.

"Mandy's grandmother is a pretty neat old lady, actually."

"Uh-huh," Lance said to keep up his side of the conversation.

"What she said made a lot of sense," Ben continued.

Lance choked on his Dew. Ben looked at him.

"What? You don't think I could change?" Ben turned and grinned at Lance.

"Just like that? Some old lady tells you to shape up and you leave on your mission the next week? Yeah, I find it a bit unbelievable," Lance said.

"Who said anything about leaving on a mission?" Ben smiled.

"I thought you just said you were going to change," Lance said confused.

"What I said was 'you don't think I could change?' I didn't say I was going to."

"So what?" Lance shook his head, still unclear. "You're not going to see your bishop?"

"Oh, heck no," Ben said. "She may have been right about a lot of things, but I'm too far down this path to change now. I'm not going out as some twenty-three-year-old missionary. Are you kidding? With all those sweet-faced, choirboy nineteen-year-olds? No way."

Ben grabbed a CD from above his visor and looked at it.

"So did you really read the Book of Mormon six times?" Lance asked.

"Yep," Ben said simply as he put the CD back and pulled out another one to inspect.

"Six times is a bit much. Why so many times?" Lance asked.

"I don't know. I just did. Partly for seminary, partly because my family read it every morning, partly because of Mandy," Ben shrugged. "I just did."

"And?"

"And what?" Ben turned quickly to look at Lance who was looking at him.

"Is it true?" Lance said.

"Probably," Ben said as he found the CD he was looking for and put it in the player, signaling the end to this exchange.

Ben turned up the volume on Black Sabbath and drowned out all chance of hearing conversations—or fire engines.

A few miles outside of Hunter, they turned. Bumping down the gravel road, they passed a campground closed for the season. They snaked down the road a mile and turned right. Just ahead, they could see dirt settling; someone was in front of them. Pulling into a clearing, a young guy with a goatee and tattoos set a six-pack of sodas down and started waving.

"My friend," Ben shouted over the music.

Lance nodded.

Ben parked and turned off the car. The CD went quiet.

Hopping out of the raised truck, Ben went to greet his friend. Lance set the almost full Dew in the cup holder and, reaching under the seat, got his gun and followed.

"Lance, Rat. Rat, Lance."

Rat put out a tattooed hand. A black widow was imprinted around his middle finger, its little legs disappearing between his other fingers.

"Rat?" Lance said.

"Raymond Adam Thomas. R.A.T."

"Oh. That works," Lance said.

"So this the gun?" Rat said, reaching for the Beretta.

Lance nodded and let him take it from his hand.

Rat turned it over a few times. He removed the clip. Looking in the chamber, he frowned.

"Got some corrosion, may or may not be able to fix it, and even if you could, it probably ain't worth it. Where'd you find it?"

"On the salt flats near Wendover," Lance said.

"Well, that accounts for the corrosion. It's an older army issue. They're pretty standard fare for the military. You can pick them up pretty cheap now-a-days." Rat handed the gun back to Lance.

Lance stuck the worthless gun in his pocket.

"Come shoot some of mine." Rat smiled at Lance and Ben and headed toward his truck.

Lance followed Ben.

After about two hours of uncomplicated bliss—just shooting guns and generally being rowdy boys, a few drops of rain fell on the pale, reddish brown downy hair that covered Lance's lower arms. He looked heavenward and was surprised to see such angry black clouds overhead.

Rat and Ben were either unaware of the pending storm or didn't care. They were taking turns shooting a semiautomatic rifle now. Taking down cans, branches, small rocks, and anything else that was not attached to the earth caused them to squeal like pigs in a mud bath.

Finally, the gun quieted down, and Ben looked at Lance. "I guess we'd better call it a day."

"What?" Lance's hearing was a bit compromised.

Ben shouted the message, using hand gestures as well.

"Yeah," Lance agreed, nodding his head because he knew Ben was as deaf as he was right then.

The rain was coming down harder anyway. Huge drops plopped on the ground and made the dust puff in response to the wet stuff on the dry stuff. A thunderous crack of lighting split the sky in the small foothills behind them.

"Lance, do you mind taking my truck back?" Ben shouted over the rapidly increasing sound of the wind and rain. "I'm gonna go with Rat; he'll bring me home later."

"Yeah, I don't care. I'm pretty sure I can find it," Lance yelled back.

"When you get to the Circle K on the right, just turn right. You should be able to find it from there; it's not far," Ben said fishing the keys out of his pocket.

"Sure," Lance said, taking the jingling set.

Ben hopped into the right side of Rat's truck. Rat got in the left side.

Lance ran toward Ben's Blazer. Grabbing the steering wheel, he pulled himself up. When he started the engine, Black Sabbath screeched out at him. He reached over, turned it down, and then off. The storm was plenty noisy enough for him.

He followed Rat's truck down the increasingly wet dirt road, staying far enough behind Rat's truck to be able to stay out of the new mud he was throwing behind his rig.

Coming up to the campground, Lance saw a large green trash bin. He threw the Blazer into park and opened the door. He ran to the closed, rusted container and lifted the black rubberized lid. Pulling the useless Beretta out of his pocket, he threw it in on a small pile of rotting refuse.

Thunder cracked again. The wind howled. The rain pelted him from the side. Above the fury of the storm, he could hear what sounded like tiny, plaintive screams of wild desert animals. He shivered at the eeriness of the tone, like a cat's cry right before she got in a fight. He backed away from the can and then turned and ran back toward the dry cab of Ben's running truck.

Chapter 13

Enin had heard both trucks earlier when they drove down the main road. She had worked in frustration in her stinky prison as she listened to the popping sounds of rifles and handguns being discharged all afternoon. She had spent her time meticulously removing the tape from around her wrists with her teeth. Once her arms were free, she took the tape off her legs. She hated that that guy had taken her shoes. She was left to stand in this filth pot of a place in her bare feet.

Initially, with her limbs freed up, she thought it would be only a matter of minutes before she was able to escape her tomb-of-stench and run down to where the shooters were. However, after an hour of pounding and kicking on the side of the outhouse, she had made no progress. Well, maybe a tiny bit. She had pulled the vent pipe out of the roof, leaving a small four-inch hole where she could see the sky. Unfortunately, all that did was make the tiny confined area smell even worse.

If she stood on the toilet seat, she could reach her small hand through the hole and wave, for as much good as that did.

Then the rain started, slowly at first, and she knew this was her last chance to catch them before they left.

As she heard the trucks leaving, she started screaming.

"Help! Somebody, please help me," she screamed through the cracks in the wooden slats.

Over and over she screamed, until one of the trucks actually stopped. The motor was still running, but the truck had stopped. It was a miracle.

"Thank you, Heavenly Father. Thank you," she quickly muttered and then started to yell once more. She straddled the toilet again and tried to scream through the vent opening.

"I'm over here . . . in the outhouse!"

The wind was picking up. Rain was pelting the side of her wooden prison. Drops that at first were just falling on her head from the leaking roof were now being pushed through the side of the outhouse.

"Help!"

No response, but she kept yelling. She was doing her part, and Heavenly Father was surely doing his.

Her yells became hysterical screams. Louder and louder she raised the pitch until the sound that came out of her was just one long primeval wail. Then, over the sound of her cracking voice, she heard the sound of the truck moving on.

"No-o-o-o!" Enin gasped. "Don't leave me. Please don't leave me." She pounded on the walls of the structure. She kicked at the base of the filthy, disgusting toilet.

She looked heavenward, and tears mixing with the rain from the leaking roof asked, "Why?"

Chapter

14

Lance pulled out onto the highway. The pounding wind and rain had not let up. It was not like any rain he had ever seen. In California, rain was rain—mostly just wet stuff falling from they sky, a function of gravity. Oh, occasionally you would get a thunderstorm with heavy rain, but even then, rain came down, not sideways. This stuff was more like Weather Channel rain—rain that did damage, rain that washed away cars and cows.

Lance tapped at the wheel on Ben's truck as he drove. He was nervous—at least he thought he was nervous. He felt agitated but didn't know why. Something was not right. He listened to the truck. Maybe it was the truck. Ben had said something about his truck not working right.

After a minute or so of listening, Lance concluded that anything that was wrong with Ben's Blazer was not going to be heard over the sound of the storm. As Lance barreled down the highway, he tried to focus on the road ahead.

"Help me," a small voice said from behind him.

Lance jumped and turned to see who was in the truck. As he did, he pulled the wheel to the right and almost left the road. The seat behind him was empty.

Lance's chest tightened; he started breathing rapidly. Blinking, he looked ahead and was surprised to see the rain letting up on his windshield. In less than a mile, the rain stopped. In front of the storm was an erratic wind, kicking up dust and tumble weeds that scuttled across the highway.

"Who's in here?" Lance said out loud.

There was no answer. Lance shook his head, as if he could get the echo of the voice out of his brain. He had heard a voice. He was sure of it. A girl's voice, full of anguish. He pulled the truck over on the side of the road but left the motor running. He undid his seat belt and crawled over the back of the seat to inspect the areas he couldn't see in his rearview mirror. Other than a spare tire, some work clothes and a few tools, the truck was empty—of people at least.

He got back in his seat and belted in. He sat there for a moment and listened with every cell of his body.

"Maybe it was the wind," he finally said to no one. He needed the sound of someone's voice to calm him down and right now his would have to do.

He reached for the audio deck and turned on Ben's CD. Black Sabbath came blaring out. He quickly reduced the volume to zero and then fiddled with the deck until the CD ejected. He couldn't do Black Sabbath right now. He had seen Ben retrieve the CD from above the visor, so he pulled that down to replace it. Ben had a ton of CDs, and Lance started to pull them out, one by one.

"EFY: The Best of Especially for Youth . . . Colors . . . Greg Simpson . . . Brian Rhodes," Lance read to himself the names of the various CDs. With the exception of this one Black Sabbath and a Kenny Chesney mix, all the CDs in Ben's collection were LDS artists. That surprised him.

He pulled the EFY one out, put it in the deck, and turned up the volume again.

Kenneth Cope's smooth voice was like a comforting blanket of familiarity. He had had this CD in Cali. He left it behind when he left the rest of his Mormon world behind him.

He hummed along with Kenneth, while he pulled back on to the road. The wind was still whipping the tumbleweeds around, but it had died down considerably.

The next song was eerily appropriate for the setting. He started to sing with the young woman on the CD.

"In the distance I can see storms begin to grow. Darkness out ahead, clouds are moving in, tempting winds they blow. Answers here, answers there, answers everywhere. Which way do I go? Then a whisper softly comes. I will let you know."

Lance stopped singing and began to listen to the words—perhaps for the first time.

"And our hearts burn within us like so many years ago. On the way to Emmeaus His words of love and hope, and our hearts burn within us as we walk down this road, take the hand of the Prince of Peace to our Father's home. I bow my head, in humility, yearning deep, reaching far, pleading with faith for direction. I want to do His will, and then a whisper softly comes. I am with you still."

Lance hit the repeat button as the song ended. He listened to the song again and then again. Something was different. He closed his eyes—maybe not the smartest thing to do as he drove down the highway—but it was only for a moment, a moment to pray.

"What do you want from me?" he asked the heavens, or more specifically, he asked his Father. "Are you there? Are you trying to tell me something?"

The only answer he got was the whistle of the wind as it passed his window and a small wash of comfort as the words *'I am with you still'* floated on the air as the song ended.

Lance let the CD continue. Maybe a good thing—maybe not. The next song caught him by complete surprise, though it shouldn't have. He knew this song and hated it. He had always hit forward when it came on. Suddenly he realized it was because it was hitting too close to home, too close to his life.

"I've gone so far from my home, seen the world and I have known so many secrets I wish now I did not know, 'cause they have crept into my heart. They have left it cold and dark and bleeding, bleeding and falling apart. And everybody used to tell me big boys don't cry. Well I've been around enough to know that was the lie that held back the tears in the eyes of a thousand prodigal sons. Well, we are children no more. We have sinned and grown old and our father waits and he watches down the road, to see his crying boys come running back to His arms and be growing young."

The words spun in Lance's mind, causing a whirlwind of emotion. If his Heavenly Father *was* answering his prayer, what was He saying?

"What do you want from me?" Lance asked aloud. He raised his voice, pleading. "Tell me! Do you think I like living like this? What do *you* want me to do?"

He remembered the voice from the backseat, so helpless.

He pushed his foot on the gas pedal and increased his speed. He had to get back to Blake's house.

In his hurry, he missed the turnoff by the Circle K. He had to go back into town and snake his way toward the house working backward.

As he pulled up the gravel driveway, he was relieved to see that Enin's Jeep was there. For some reason, he had been thinking of her this whole time. Maybe she would have the explanation for him of what was going on. She was religious— no maybe that was the wrong word. She seemed spiritual, connected. Maybe she could explain it.

He pulled around the back and parked the truck. The back door to the house was slightly ajar. He bounded up the steps calling out her name.

"Enin," he shouted.

As he pushed on the kitchen door, a few flies flew out.

What dork left the door open? he wondered as he surveyed the mess before him, trying to make sense of the chair sprawled across the floor.

Flies were everywhere.

"Enin?" He called again, this time his voice rising with the panic he was beginning to feel. "Enin? You in here?" He walked down the hallway. Clothes were scattered everywhere, but not like someone was doing laundry. These clothes were mostly folded and tossed randomly about. He pushed the bedroom door open.

More flies were buzzing in and out of a can of Sprite that Blake had left on the desk the night before. All the drawers in the desk were torn out and on the floor. One was broken. Blake's upper mattress was on the floor. His mattress had been pulled off the frame and lay haphazardly against the back wall of the bedroom.

As he tried to take in the mess, he noticed the bunkie board that used to be under his mattress was shredded and the dog tags were missing. Someone had ripped off the entire fabric of the bunkie board. Someone was looking for something and had been pretty aggressive about it.

He didn't have to be a rocket scientist to figure out that they were looking for the Beretta; he was sure of that. But how would they know to look here? And where was Enin? He slowly backed out of the room and turned toward the kitchen.

He stepped over clothes and numbly walked toward the phone to call 911. This was all his fault. He had brought the stupid gun here and put all these people through this. He picked up the phone. No dial tone. He clicked the button a few times, but still there was no dial tone. This was like a bad B movie, except he was the star.

He walked, and then ran, outside to the barn.

"Enin!" he shouted, but somewhere deep inside he knew she wasn't here. If she was here, he was sure he could have felt her.

He turned toward Enin's Jeep. As he passed by the front porch, he noticed Enin's lunch box purse on the second step.

Now he knew. She was gone, and it wasn't by choice, because he knew as well as anyone could, Enin would never leave her *Dukes of Hazard* purse behind.

He ran and got the purse. Throwing it in Ben's truck, he realized that whoever wanted the gun had taken Enin. To get Enin back meant he had to get the gun back. He ran back in the kitchen. He had to get the gun before someone emptied the trash out at the campground. He had to get the gun. It was all he could think of.

He scribbled on the back of some junk mail. "I think Enin's been kidnapped. The phone's not working. Someone call the police. I went to get the gun. Lance."

He shoved the envelope next to the door jam and closed the door. Whoever came home first would see it.

Throwing the Blazer into reverse, he kicked up gravel. He could see the black clouds racing toward Magna, the sheets of rain a black band of vertical horror. He was going to have to go back into the advancing storm.

He sped back toward town. He barely stopped for signal lights or signs. At one intersection, he got air—which was an amazing thing to do with a Blazer. He didn't care if the police saw him, he was hoping they would so they could follow him, but on this particular Sunday afternoon not a car was in sight. Oh, one maybe, a gray Taurus made a left in front of him as he passed by the gas station.

Screaming out of town, he hit the band of incoming rain doing almost 100 mph. He thought about Enin as he passed the "Hunter—3 miles" sign. Where was she? He slowed down as he passed through Hunter, but only to sixty. Then he immediately went back up to triple digits, pushing at the rain ahead of him.

A mile out of Hunter the rain stopped. It was still windy, but even that died down as he moved farther from the freakish storm. He turned so suddenly at the quarry turn-off that he spun the Blazer in the loose, wet gravel. Breathing hard, he corrected his course and bumped up the road to the trash can.

He hopped out and left the truck running. He pulled up on the old rubbery lid and threw it back out of his way. He tried to reach in and get his gun, but it was just a bit too far for him to grab. He was going to have to get in the beat-up old container to retrieve the gun.

He threw one leg over the side, then the other, and slid into the can. He landed on a soft, stinky mound of trash. He got his gun and stuffed it into his pants pocket. As he was pulling himself out, the truck started to sputter and shake.

"What the heck?" Lance said. He got to the truck just as it quit.

He got in the truck and tried the key again. The starter turned over and over. It wasn't getting any gas. He pulled the hood latch and got out of the truck. He popped the hood and jiggled a few components.

He went back to the cab, leaned over the seat, and tried to start it. As he was leaning on his right elbow listening, while cranking the engine, his nose brushed the steering wheel. He glanced up instinctively and noticed the red check-gauge light was on. His eyes had to adjust to the different gauge system, but sure enough, the fuel gauge needle sat in the red zone.

"Oh, you *have* got to be kidding me!" he muttered as he pulled himself out of the cab.

He was out of gas. In his rush here, he had never thought to check.

He looked up. "So much for divine intervention," he said as he looked around for what to do next. He was at the road that led to the campground. He thought he had seen a sign that said it was closed earlier, but maybe he was mistaken. Maybe there were late-season campers still there, or better yet, maybe there was a phone he could use to call someone—anyone.

He pulled the keys from the ignition, dropped the hood, and locked the truck where it sat. It wouldn't be hard for someone to figure out what direction he went should anyone happen by this way. The campground sign was riddled with bullet holes, but he could read the half-mile part okay. He started walking down the part dirt, part gravel, part old pavement road. He thought of Rat and Ben and wondered if they had gotten back to the house yet. *Had anyone called the police?* He could have kicked himself for not stopping in town and doing it himself, but he really thought he would have been on his way home by now.

As he walked around the bend, he could see that it might be a half mile by road, but if he crossed over a field of boulders and went up a smallish hill, he could cut some time off the trip. He could see some scrubby trees on the top of a small hill. That must be the campground. From where he was, he couldn't see any campers.

The ground was wet and soggy as he passed through to the boulders, where he could make his way okay. The boulders were still a bit wet but not slippery like the kind you find in a creek. He balanced from one rock to another.

As he moved closer to the campground, he thought he heard someone yelling, but the sound was very faint. He moved toward the sound, which was definitely getting louder—but at the same time not so loud if you weren't paying attention. It would be easy to miss.

As he scurried up the last hill, he thought he knew that someone was in the campground. The sound he heard intermittently was sort of like kids playing in the distance, except in this case there was only one voice and one kid.

At the top of the hill, when he could actually see the campground in the distance, he was surprised to see no one. There were a few trees, a few camping spots, and a beat-up outhouse. There was no phone booth and no people. He lowered his head and turned to leave.

"Help me!" Lance heard, no felt, the tiny voice from behind him. It was *the* voice. The one in the car. The little helpless voice of someone in trouble. He swung his body around and looked at the campground again.

He scanned the scene again: scrubby, shadeless trees; worn-out picnic benches; an outhouse with a small bird fluttering on the top. *Wait, that wasn't a bird. What the heck was it?* He walked closer to the campground and squinted in the setting sun. It looked like there was a small hand sticking out of the top of the wooden structure.

"Help me," a voice hoarse with exhaustion cried. "Please, help me."

Lance ran toward the wooden structure.

"Hello?" Lance shouted to the building as he ran. "Hello? Do you need help?"

As he got closer, he could see the outhouse had silver bands of duct tape wrapped around it.

"Yes." The little hand pulled back into its cage. "Yes. Someone locked me in here. I can't open the door," the voice said, weak and tight with fatigue.

Lance grabbed one end of the freshly applied tape and ran around the wooden house two times, and it was off. Lance pulled the door open, and Enin collapsed into his arms.

Chapter

15

"What the!" Lance gasped as Enin fell forward into his arms. He wasn't sure if she had actually fainted or tumbled from exhaustion. He caught her and held her tight. He was shocked and grateful at the same time. She was soft and venerable. Her hair was matted with rain and sweat and smelled of outhouse. He noticed her bare feet, little pieces of toilet paper sticking to the sides of them. She didn't smell too good, but she looked wonderful to him. He realized now that his anxiety all along had been over her, but until that very moment, he couldn't have articulated that thought.

Apparently she did not know that she was in his arms. She was limp and quiet. She was breathing air in gulps. Her head down, she mumbled a thank-you into his chest.

"Enin?" Lance said softly.

Enin looked up, surprise registering on her face.

"Lance? What . . . what are you doing here?" She looked

around. "Where's Ben?"

Lance shook his head. "He's not here. You're stuck with me."

"I don't understand," Enin said, but she did not let go of him.

"You and me both. Can you tell me what happened?"

"Some crazy guy came looking for a gun Blake supposedly had. He tore the house apart. Then, when he couldn't find it, he took me and left me here. He has a gun, Lance. He went back to town looking for Blake, I think."

Lance took this information in. He wasn't sure if he should mention the gun in question was his.

"Why are you here? How did you know where to find me?"

How indeed, Lance thought.

"Long story," Lance said after a moment's hesitation. "I think right now we have to get out of here."

Enin looked around. "Where are my shoes?" she asked practically.

"I don't know. Should they be here?"

Enin shrugged, "Well, I thought he set them next to the outhouse."

"He must have taken them with him. Did he say when he was coming back?"

She shook her head and then looked around as she began to get her bearings.

"What did you drive? Did you fix your truck?" Enin asked, confused.

"I have Ben's."

"Ben's?" She said, not understanding.

"Part of that long story I have to tell you sometime, but right now we have bigger problems."

Enin shook her head. "I don't think I can handle any more problems today."

"I understand, but unfortunately we still have a few issues."

"Like what?" Enin finally pushed herself away from Lance's chest. She teetered for a moment, and he put both hands on her waist to steady her.

"In my rush to get back here . . ." Lance started.

"Back? That was you shooting this afternoon?"

"Yeah. Me, Ben, and some guy named Rat. Anyway, in my rush, I didn't notice Ben's truck was almost empty. I ran out of gas at the entrance to this campground. I only came up here to find a phone."

"So are you saying we can't drive out of here?" Enin's voice begged for this not to be so.

Lance lowered his eyes; tears welled up in Enin's.

"Enin, we have to get out of here. This guy, the crazy one, could come back at any time. He is not going to like what he finds."

"I know." Enin took in a big breath and squared her shoulders as best she could.

"Well, we can't stay here." He looked around the campground. "I think to buy us a little time we can tape the outhouse shut again and maybe . . ." He looked at the outhouse closely. "Maybe push some of the boards off on the top. It will look like you took off alone—but he won't know how long ago."

"Okay," Enin said. "There's this old mining cave we could go to. It's sort of by the quarry. I've been spelunking in it a few times."

"How far?"

"Maybe a mile if we stay off the main road, but . . ." Enin looked at the deepening red sunset and sighed. "It'll be dark soon."

"Right, which is why we have to move fast." He stepped into the outhouse, coughed a bit, and then stood on the toilet deck. He noticed the wooden roof was rotted away in one spot. Pushing hard on the roof, one board gave way and then another. He only pushed out two. Enin was small; that's all she would have needed to get out.

"Yuck," he said as he stepped out.

"Yeah," Erin agreed.

Lance picked up the silver tape that was lying on the concrete pad that surrounded the outhouse. He carefully straightened it out and resealed the former prison. The duct tape was still mostly sticky, and when he stepped back to inspect his work, it looked approximately like it did when he first got there. He turned to Enin. "You know Ben better than I do. Does he keep a flashlight in his rig?"

"Yeah, he does. One of those little expensive ones."

"Okay, here's the plan—and keep in mind I am making this up as I go. I go back to the truck and get what I can; then we go to this cave. We are going to have to stay off the main roads and also out of the mud. We can't afford to leave tracks. He probably won't be able to track us until morning. By then, hopefully, we will have figured out what to do. Okay?"

"Okay, except for the part where you leave me here alone. I'm coming with you."

Lance looked down at Enin's bare feet.

"You can't leave me here, Lance. You just can't." Her voice had a slight quiver to it.

"All right." He squatted down, his back to her. "Hop on."

Enin put her arms around his neck and her legs around his waist. Lance stood up and started back toward the truck. He was careful to not to leave any tracks; he kept to either the scrubby grass or dryer gravel on the road. He walked on rocks when he could.

It took longer to get back there than either of them expected. As the last of the shadowy light in the west sank behind the horizon, they reached the Blazer. Lance set Enin down and opened the truck. The overhead lights went on.

"Where's the flashlight?" Lance said as he crawled into the truck.

"Under the backseat, in his tool box, I think."

Lance leaned over the front seat and reached under the

backseat, feeling around for a tool box. He first pulled out one Sketcher and then another. While the shoes were clearly too big for Enin, at least she could hobble along. He was grateful to see that each shoe contained a sock, a used one, but you count your blessings when you can. He set them on the seat and kept reaching. After a moment, he pulled out a slender metal box. It seemed too small to be a toolbox, but upon inspection, that's exactly what it was. It was a compact version of a complete tool set. Sort of like what a Gerber knife is to a drawer full of tools. And sure enough, there was a flashlight in it. He then crawled completely over the seat and looked in the back where the spare tire was. He was pleased to find an old greasy sweatshirt and a rope. He would take both.

"Are you almost done?" Enin's voice came from just inside the truck. He looked at her and nodded. Handing her the stuff, he pulled himself over and got out of the truck. As an afterthought, he reached back in and got his almost full Mountain Dew and Enin's purse from on the floorboards, where it had come to rest after his spinout.

Lance handed the surprised Enin her purse and the Dew. "I'm not sure what we can do about the truck. I mean, we can't move it. We can't hide it. I guess we'll just lock it up and leave."

"Where'd you get this?" Enin said as she held up her *Dukes of Hazard* purse.

"On the steps of Blake's house. That's how I knew you were in trouble."

"Is this part of that long story you have yet to tell me?"

"Uh-huh. Let's get moving though, and while I'm sure you want me to start right now with the story, I think it's best if we just walk as quietly as we can, for as long as we can. We don't know when this creep will get back, and I don't want him knowing where to look for us any sooner that he has to."

Enin nodded.

"Oh, I got you these." Lance held up the Sketchers.

"Ben's shoes." She took them and held them to her chest.

With that, she started to sob. He reached out and pulled her close to him, although the shoes were still between them. She didn't resist. He let her cry herself out before he reached for the shoes.

He lifted her up and placed her on the driver's seat of the truck. He was eager to leave, but he also knew he couldn't push Enin right now. *Heavenly Father, don't let that creep come back now. A few more minutes is all I'm asking.*

He took one bare foot in his hands and used his T-shirt to clean off the mud and debris. He noticed the angry red bands around her ankle. He had noticed them around her wrists earlier. He felt the weight of the powerless gun in his pocket. He shook his head. It was a good thing that Beretta didn't work right now, or this creep might be the cause of him going to jail for a very, very long time.

As he pulled the sock onto her foot, Enin winced in pain. He quickly pulled it down below her ankle. He put on the shoe and tied it as tight as he could under the circumstances. Then he started the procedure all over again with the other foot.

"Do you want this sweatshirt?" Lance asked, holding out the greasy work shirt.

"Uh-huh," was all she said. It was clear that she was exhausted, but they had to get moving.

"Can you walk okay in these?" He said as he set her on the ground.

She took a few tentative steps. "Yeah. Thanks."

"I think we should carry some of Ben's stuff. Can you carry the Mountain Dew and the flashlight, and I'll carry the rest?"

"Sure."

"Do you want some of the Dew?" He pointed to the bottle in her hand.

"I normally don't drink Mountain Dew," Enin said flatly.

"Well, you normally don't get kidnapped and locked in an outhouse for a day. I think under the circumstances the Lord will forgive you if you drink a caffeinated soda."

Enin laughed weakly, nodded her head, and took the soda. She gulped half of it down, not even stopping for a breath. When she was done, she wiped at her mouth with the back of her hand.

"Better?"

"Yes, thank you," she said meekly. Lance could tell Enin had been traumatized, because she was very weak and compliant—traits not normally associated with Enin.

"I also have a little food with me." He reached down in his pockets and pulled out his booty: one unopened Snickers, one half-eaten Baby Ruth, and half a bag of cashews. "Your choice."

Enin took the Snickers and opened it up.

Lance locked the truck, pocketed the keys, and then looked down at Enin's clown shoes.

"Which way did you say the cave was?"

She pointed east, away from the main road.

"I have another idea. Let's go back toward the main road leaving two, very distinctive sets of large footprints, and then double back to the cave through the rocks and bushes. With any luck, he won't tie the truck to your escaping. Maybe he'll just think someone ran out of gas and had to walk back to the main road.

"Uh, what if he comes back and sees us?" Enin asked.

"I'm not saying it isn't a risk, but walking straight to the cave will lead him right to us. I don't think we have a choice. We'll just have to trust in the powers that be."

"You mean, trust in Heavenly Father?" Enin asked pointedly, giving him the first hint of her old self.

Chapter

16

Because of the break-in last night, Ben was not overly surprised to see the flashing lights of a sheriff's vehicle in his driveway when Rat dropped him off. Rat didn't much like the sheriff's department, so he just let Ben off near the mailbox and sped away. Ben was, however, taken back to see his parents' red Astro van parked behind Enin's Jeep—now that was unusual.

As he walked up the dark, long gravel drive to the house, Blake came running out of the house toward him.

"Where've you been, man? Your parents are freaking out."

"What?" Ben was instantly alert. "What's the matter with my parents?"

"Not your parents. Enin."

"Enin?" He looked from Blake, to the Jeep, to the house.

"Where's Enin? What's the matter with her?" he said, panic rising in his voice.

"She's been kidnapped," Blake said.

"You are flippin' kidding me, man."

"No, I swear. Whoever came last night must have come back this afternoon when Enin was here. The police think he, or she, or they, took her." Blake stumbled on the words as they came out.

Running toward the house, Ben took the three porch steps in one leap and pushed on the partially opened front door with such force that it crashed into the old lathe and plaster, sending a family picture Enin had put on the wall crashing to the floor.

"Where's Enin?" he screamed at the collective party in the room.

"Ben," his father said, stepping toward him. "We don't know. We were hoping she was with you."

"I haven't seen her since yesterday. I did talk to her this morning, but she only said she had homework to do. What's going on? Why do you think she's been kidnapped?" Ben asked, noticing his mother sitting in a chair, rocking back and forth.

"All we have right now is this note from someone named Lance," his dad said, pointing to the local sheriff who was wearing a black suit and tie and holding a Ziploc bag that contained an envelope.

Ben crossed the room. "Can I see it?" Ben held out his hand.

In response, Sheriff Butler held it up but didn't let Ben touch it.

Ben could read the hastily penciled note: "I think Enin's been kidnapped. The phone's not working. Someone call the police. I went to get the gun. Lance."

"What gun is he talking about?" Sheriff Butler asked.

"I don't know. Maybe the one he found out on the salt flats. He took it with him today to show to Rat . . . but that doesn't make any sense. Why would he go to get it? He had it when we left."

"We need to start at the beginning," Sheriff Butler said. "Who is Lance?"

"Blake's friend," he said, looking at Blake to confirm this. "Blake towed his 4Runner in a few days ago because he busted his tranny out near Wendover. He didn't have anywhere to go, so Blake invited him to stay here. He's a nice enough kid. He's sort of Mormon and came from Sacramento, I think."

Sheriff Butler nodded and wrote something down.

As Ben began to breathe more evenly, he scanned the living room. In his haste, he hadn't noticed the disarray.

"What happened here?" Ben said, pointing to the mess that extended down the hall.

"Apparently, someone broke in and was looking for something," the sheriff said.

"The same people who broke in last night?" Ben asked.

"Probably."

"We only thought it was kids, Bishop." Ben's voice was on the edge of tears. "They went through the cars in the barn, but they didn't take anything."

"Jared and Blake told me about it this afternoon. I didn't think it was anything either, Ben, or I would have come over right away."

"When did you get here?" Ben asked.

"Blake called me at home when he got here an hour ago. We tried calling your cell earlier, but it kept going to your voice mail."

Ben pulled his cell phone out of his pocket and flipped it open. There were no bars in the battery symbol on his phone. He lowered his head. "I didn't charge it last night."

The sheriff nodded. "So you and your friend Rat went out shooting?"

"Uh-huh. The quarry outside of Hunter."

"And he had this gun with him?"

"Yeah, but he never used it. It didn't work. It was corroded or something. We were using Rat's."

"So you never saw him shoot the gun?"

"No. What's the gun got to do with it?"

"We don't know. But we also don't know much about this Lance friend of yours."

"You don't think Lance had anything to do with this," Ben said, surprised, thinking back to his sister's paranoia about Lance.

"We haven't come to any conclusions yet. All we know is that Enin is not here, but her Jeep is. We know she never showed up to go visiting teaching, and Lance thinks she was kidnapped. That doesn't mean she was, but we also don't know who broke into your house or why. The two events may or may not be related."

Ben paced back and forth in the small living room.

"So what do we do now? Don't you call in the FBI or something when someone gets kidnapped?"

"It depends. We don't know for sure she was. Remember, Lance just thinks she was. He may have been jumping to conclusions based on the break-in. She could be out with a friend."

"Well, have we called all her friends?"

At this point, Ben's mom spoke. "I called Liz and Stephanie. They saw her at church but haven't heard from her since."

"Well, what about her other friends?"

"I don't know their numbers," his mom said weakly.

"What about her cell phone? Has anybody called that?"

"She left it home on the charger. It rang once this afternoon; that's the only reason I knew it was at home," Ben's dad said.

"Where is it now?"

"Here." His mom pulled the cell phone out of a large bag.

"Blake, go through all her numbers and see if anyone has seen her." Ben took the phone from his mom and handed it to Blake. Blake took the little silver phone and stepped onto the porch.

The sheriff let Ben chat with his family and wrote down some more information in his notebook.

Blake came back in the house with the phone held out in front of him. "Somebody might want to talk to Suzanne. She thinks she may have seen Enin earlier today in town, but she's not sure."

Ben and the sheriff both reached for the phone. Ben deferred to the law and sat on the edge of the chair next to his mom, where he rested his hand on her shoulder.

"Hello? This is Sheriff Butler . . . Oh, hi, Suzie . . . We don't know, that's what we're trying to figure out . . . Uh-huh . . . Are you sure it was a Taurus?"

Ben jumped up off the chair at the word Taurus. "Oh my gosh, the gray Taurus. He cut off some guy in front of us in town this afternoon. Lance saw it too. He said the girl inside looked like Enin. Oh, shhhh . . ." Ben's hand flew to his mouth.

"Hold on, Suzanne," the sheriff said into the phone as he looked at Ben. "Are you sure?"

"I'm sure Lance thought it was Enin. We talked about girls in ponytails afterward," Ben said rapidly.

"Did you actually see the car?"

"Yeah, we were coming out of the McDonald's, and the Taurus cut off some old man."

"Hold that thought, Ben," Sheriff Butler said.

"Suzanne? Do you happen to remember what color the Taurus was . . . Uh-huh . . . Are you sure? California license plates . . . okay, but you don't remember the number . . . Uh-huh . . . Listen, can you stay by your phone? I may be sending out someone to take a statement a little later . . . Uh-huh . . . Absolutely, Suzie, prayer is always a good idea." He shut the little flip phone and handed it back to Blake. "Keep calling, Blake," the sheriff instructed.

Ben's dad had come and taken Ben's place next to his mother. Her face was in her hands. She resumed rocking back and forth.

"So now what?" Ben asked the sheriff.

The sheriff sighed. "I'm afraid we may be calling in the

FBI. Right now, I want all of you to leave the house. We are going to have to dust for prints and cordon off the area. I suggest that you all go to the Woodson home for now. I'll call you when I have more information." He then looked at Ben's mother, who was watching him intently. "I promise, Sister Woodson, I'll call personally when we find out anything." Turning to Ben, he said, "Ben, I need you to stay here. I have a few more questions, and I'm going to need your help in sorting through some of the stuff in the house and later in the barn, okay?"

"Sure," Ben said.

"Are we going to be able to come back tonight?" Blake asked the sheriff.

"I wouldn't count on it."

"Well, what about taking some stuff with us?" He nodded toward Jared, who had been quiet the entire time. "Is that okay?"

The sheriff sucked in a deep breath between clenched teeth.

"I take it that's a no."

"I'm sorry Blake. We don't know what we're dealing with yet."

"Blake, you and Jared come over to our house. We'll put you up for as long as this takes. Ben will follow later. Right, Ben?" Ben knew his dad had added this last part for his mother.

"Absolutely, Dad, absolutely."

Chapter
17

Enin walked toward the main road, Ben's shoes leaving big, gooey prints in the mud. They were trying to walk fast and hard, so the prints would be clearly visible to anyone who passed by. As the sky darkened in the west, the random lightning from the departing storm in the northeast provided more and more needed light to guide them along the unlit road. At first, they kept to the more muddy parts of the road that led toward the highway, but when they came to a turn in the road, Lance stopped.

"How 'bout we just keep walking, instead of making the turn? It will look like we took a shortcut to the highway," he said to Enin, who had been walking at his side.

"Yeah, that's fine."

"Can you find the cave if we're not on the road?"

"I think so; as long as I can keep the road in sight, I should be fine."

They both stepped off into the rugged terrain and walked another ten feet, careful to leave prints.

"Okay, now the game is walk and don't leave any evidence," Lance said.

"Walking awkwardly in these shoes is not a problem; being nimble might be." Enin said looking down at the mud-globbed Sketchers.

Initially, they hopped from rock outcropping to rock outcropping but keeping the gravel road in sight. After they were about 200 feet east of Ben's truck, Lance started to track back toward the rutty road. They stayed on the side of it for another quarter mile when Enin stopped.

"I think it's this way." She pointed south.

"Lead on." Lance said.

A half mile in, Enin left the safety of the established trail and headed south, toward some low hills in the distance.

She had the flashlight but only used it in the more rocky sections of the path. Between the distant lightning and the full moon rising in the east, intermittently peeking out from the clouds, she was able to make her way closer to the mine shaft in question. Lance followed dutifully, a footstep behind her. He hadn't said a word since they had left the road.

She was truly grateful for his presence, but the further away they got from the main road the more questions she had. Why Lance? It didn't make sense that he would be the one to rescue her. Her initial reaction was relief that he was here, but why hadn't the Lord sent a more well-known ally to help her in her time of distress? Why not Blake, Jared, or Ben, or one of her other brothers? She didn't even know this guy whose arms she had recently been in.

She was exhausted yet fully awake—probably a function of the caffeine in the Mountain Dew.

"Are we okay to talk now?" Enin asked Lance.

"Sure. I doubt anyone but the owls are going to hear us now. We're probably half a mile in, wouldn't you say?"

"Yeah, about that," Enin agreed.

"So I guess you want me to tell you how it is I came to be your rescuer instead of your brother or someone else."

It was if he had read her mind. She blushed and shivered. Of course, Lance couldn't have seen the color in her face.

He asked in response to her sudden shaking, "You cold?"

"Ah, no. I'm fine. Just a little tired."

"Well, you have every right to be."

"So?" Enin said.

"Oh, the long story. Well, you know that my truck broke down outside of Wendover, right?"

"Yeah."

"Okay, so what you don't know is that as I was waiting for Blake to come and get me, I found this gun and a set of dog tags on the salt flats."

Enin spun around.

"It's your gun? The guy thinks it's Blake's. He's out there right now looking for Blake, to get the gun back."

Lance lowered his head. "Don't remind me. I am fully aware of the problems this stupid gun has caused." He looked down at his pants and patted his lower pocket.

Enin followed his gaze; then he took a step back in horror.

"You have the gun? Now? On you?" The words tumbled out of her mouth.

"Yeah, but don't worry. The gun is basically useless; it got corroded in the salt flats and won't hurt anyone."

"Except for the people who have it—like us!" Enin shouted.

"Hold on and don't shout, for Pete's sake. That's why I came back here. When we were done shooting this afternoon, I tossed the gun into that trash container next to Ben's truck back there." He motioned with his head toward the main road.

"When I got home and saw the house torn apart and the dog tags missing, it didn't take a rocket scientist to figure out somebody was looking for the gun. I came back to get it. Then I was going to take it to the police and turn it in."

"Did you call the police?"

Lance shook his head. "No. The phone was dead at Blake's. I figured I would come out here, get the gun, and get back. I knew the guy who wanted the gun must have taken you too, but at the time, I was only looking for the gun. Finding you was a happy accident."

"So you weren't looking for me?" Enin put her head down.

"Well, not yet. Not officially. But I did hear you."

"What do you mean, you heard me?"

"Okay, this is the part of the story that gets a little confusing for me, and I'm hoping you can explain it."

"Go on," Enin said. They were now walking side by side.

"When I dropped the gun off the first time, I thought I heard someone or something screaming. I convinced myself it was just the storm—"

"I—" Enin said, interrupting.

"Wait, let me finish the whole thing. Then you can ask questions or comment," Lance said.

Enin nodded.

"Anyway, I thought it was the storm, but then in the car I heard a voice. It said, 'Help me.' It totally freaked me out. I'm not used to hearing voices. I even stopped the truck because I thought someone was in the Blazer with me. I'll admit at the time I didn't know it was yours, probably because I'm not as familiar with your voice as other people might be, but the second time you said it, back in the outhouse, I knew it was your voice I heard in the truck."

He paused only to take a breath.

"Another thing that happened was that when I got to the house, I knew you were gone. I couldn't feel you. I can't explain it, but I knew you were gone. So I left a note for the guys to call the police and then I raced back here." Lance stopped and looked directly at Enin. "So why is that, Enin? Why could I hear you and feel that you weren't there? I hardly know you."

"Because I prayed you here," Enin said simply, answering

both their questions at once and then pointing to a darkened crevice in the side of the hill. "The cave is right up there."

"Well, let's get up there. We can get some sleep and figure out what to do from there."

As they ascended the hill, they passed an old abandoned station wagon. Long past its prime, it had been rolled a few times and used for target practice. It was in its righted position, but there was no glass visible in the windows, the hood was missing, along with the left passenger door. The wheels and tires were nowhere to be seen.

Enin shone the little mag light on the side of the hill and was startled to find a door—a large metal grate—had been installed over the mine entrance, effectively keeping out all visitors. Tears welled up in her eyes as she looked at Lance.

"I take it that wasn't there before," Lance said resignedly.

Enin just shook her head.

"Okay, we'll go to plan B."

"What is plan B?" Enin asked.

"We sleep in that old abandoned car. I doubt if our crazy friend is going to go hunting for us tonight."

"Actually, I think you are probably right. He doesn't go anywhere without his dumb map, and this place is not on any map that I know of."

They turned and walked back toward the car.

"Let me see the flashlight, please," Lance said as he held out his hand.

Shining a light in the car caused a flurry of bug activity. Spiders in winsome webs moved away from the light. Little black bugs of some sort scurried under the seats. Enin was witness to all this activity and backed away from the car.

"I don't think so, Lance."

"Enin, we can't sleep on the ground. It's too wet still, and we don't know that we aren't going to have more rain tonight. It's a little protection at least."

"Lance, I just spent the better part of today in an outhouse with a thousand flies and spiders. I am *not* going to spend my night with them as well. No. Period. You'll have to come up with plan C."

"Okay, let's go back to the mine. Maybe we can just rest under a ledge of some sort."

Enin answered by turning and walking back up the hill. When they got to the actual mine, they could see the lock—which they assumed was keeping the door in place—was actually broken. With very little effort, Lance was able to remove it and open the door. Shining the light in before him, he stepped into the old mine. It was cool but dry. Along the side of the entrance was a wooden bench of sorts. Something the miners must have used while waiting to go down the vertical shafts into the bowels of the earth.

"Better," Enin said.

"Enin?" Lance said.

She turned quickly to look at him. His voice was suddenly choked with emotion.

"What?" Enin asked, puzzled.

"Thank you."

"For what?" Enin said.

"For praying me here. Can you do it again? Can you pray for Blake. I never meant for any of this to happen. You know that, don't you?"

Enin nodded her head and then sat down next to him on the bench. She took his hands in hers, and he responded by intertwining his fingers with hers. They both bowed heads.

After a sweet, sincere prayer for guidance and safety for their friends and family, she started to pull her hands away, but Lance tightened his grip just a bit. Enin's hands stayed still.

"I have a question," Enin said at last.

"What?"

"It's about your family."

Lance's fingers stiffened a little, and he started to pull his hands away.

"No," Enin said simply and held tight to his hands.

"I don't like to talk about my family."

"I could tell," Enin said.

"So why would you want me to? What possible gain could you get out of it, besides idle curiosity?" Lance said honestly.

"I have a feeling that nothing happening right now is idle."

Lance nodded.

"So what do you want to know about my family?" Lance said after a moment of silence.

"Why you get so angry when someone brings it up?"

Lance shrugged and then spoke. "I don't know if I get angry as much as frustrated. My family is different."

"Lots of families are different, both in and out of the Church."

"Yeah, but my family is different by even outside the Church standards—and when you add the whole 'Families-Can-Be-Together-Forever' to the mix, you have a whole new definition of dysfunction."

"I don't understand."

"Exactly, and that is why I don't like to talk about it."

"But I want to. I want to understand."

Lance sighed.

"Please," Enin pleaded.

"Enin, to start with my mother got pregnant by some guy in San Diego. She claimed she never knew anything but his first name: Lance."

"Your mother named you after him?"

"Yeah, which always seemed odd to me since he left her to raise me alone. But then again, he did die in the gulf, so maybe it was out of respect."

Enin nodded.

"So this guy, my father, was in the military. My mother was very vague on the subject, but this I do know: he was Mormon; my mother was not."

"Okay, so your mom got pregnant and wasn't married. That's not that unusual. It happens here too. People aren't perfect, but they repent and get on with their lives. Your mom did. You said so."

"Yes, I said my mother did eventually marry. When I was about two, my mother met another LDS guy, William Andrews. She married him and had two more kids: my younger brother who's seventeen, and my sister who's sixteen. I guess they were always planning on having him adopt me, but before they got around to it, my mom was killed in an automobile accident."

"Oh, how awful." Enin squeezed Lance's hands just a little tighter.

"Yeah, well, I was six. I only have the vaguest of memories of my mom. Anyway, after my mom died, the only dad I ever knew married Sandy, who is not Mormon, but then my stepdad couldn't adopt me because my mother had passed away before she signed the papers. So my birth name was Morris, but I went by Andrews for most of my life, like my half-brother and half-sister. Looking back, I'm not sure how they got me enrolled in school that way, but they did, and for most of my life, in school at least, I have gone by the last name of Andrews, even though it's not my real name. My driver's license and name at church are both Morris—but most people know me as Lance Andrews."

Enin leaned her head on Lance's shoulder, and it sent a chill through him. He paused for a moment to catch a sharp breath and then continued.

"Well anyway, my stepdad marries Sandy and then they had two more kids, Jason, who is fifteen and Carole Ann, who is fourteen. Okay, so by then I had four Andrews siblings—two of whom I am biologically related to, two of whom I am not. Unfortunately, my stepdad got pancreatic cancer when I was eleven, and six weeks after the diagnosis, he died."

Enin sat up. "You're kidding."

Lance looked at her, his eyebrows furrowing.

Enin shook her head in apology. "Okay, clearly you're not kidding, but that is just terrible. I feel so sorry for you."

"Hold on, Enin, there's more. You wanted the whole enchilada, and I'm not stopping now."

"Go on," Enin said as she laid her head, once again, on Lance's shoulder.

"So there I was, living with Sandy and my brothers and sisters, and Sandy met Joseph Raintree, a nice enough guy who has a couple of kids of his own. Wait, did I mention that Sandy had kids before she married my dad? Well, she did—two, but they lived with their dad. So we are really a family of seven kids, depending on the holiday. Anyway, back to Raintree. So Sandy met Raintree at some Parents Without Partners meeting. Raintree is Mormon, very Mormon. His wife died of cancer, so he and Sandy both had something in common. The next thing I knew, I'm a Raintree, and I have three more half-siblings. That makes seven of us at home and the two of Sandy's who don't live with us. Well, obviously, I'm not really a Raintree. I didn't change my name or anything, but Raintree is pretty active in the Church, so when we all show up to church people think of us collectively as the Raintree kids. You have to understand that up until this time, I just attended church occasionally, when someone from our ward noticed the "inactive family" and came and took the poor kids to primary or mutual activities."

"That sounds kind of harsh," Enin said, so close to Lance's ear that her breath was warm and sweet on his cheek.

"It *was* harsh, Enin. I don't think you guys raised out here in Happyville have a clue how difficult it is to be raised in such a weird family and fit in at church."

"Go on," was all Enin said.

"So living with Raintree really did change Sandy. She joined the Church and became really active. Before you knew it, they had two more kids: Coco and Casandra. We were at ten kids. Well, Joseph wanted us all to go to the temple and be sealed as one happy family. A worthy goal, to be sure, but there was one little complication—me."

"How so?"

"Remember back when my mom died? I was never legally adopted by Andrews, so I could not be legally adopted by Sandy like my other siblings, who were later legally adopted by Raintree. I couldn't be sealed. So on the big happy day, I sat outside the Los Angeles Temple while the only family I'd ever known was in there getting sealed."

Enin stroked Lance's arm and then sighed and shivered. Lance untangled one hand and moved his arm around her. She snuggled up next to him.

"I was a teenager at the time, and the stake president told me that when I was eighteen I could choose for myself whom I wanted to be sealed to, because at that time I would be legally able to make decisions for myself. Don't get me wrong. Joseph is a great man, a great stepfather—but he wasn't my dad. And Sandy? As wonderful as she was, she was never my mother. I couldn't see being sealed to either of them by the time I turned eighteen. I didn't know what I wanted. I suppose I wanted to be sealed to my real mother—but who would she be sealed to? Andrews? And if she was sealed to him, then what about his kids he had with Sandy, who were adopted by Joseph? See how complicated it all gets? When the time came for me to think about a mission, I was one confused puppy. I didn't know how to preach the concept of a forever family when I would never be a part of one myself."

Enin sat up and looked at Lance. The mine was mostly dark, but the moon was getting higher in the sky and threw a faint hint of light in the cave. "That's not true, Lance. In the end, the only part of your forever family that you really have to worry about is your wife. Look, my mom and dad are sealed to each other and to us, but my brothers and I aren't going to be living with them as single children through the eternities. They are going to be together, and someday I'm going to be with my husband. I suppose we'll visit, and being sealed gives us that opportunity, but I don't get the impression that my father will be like my dad is now. Haven't you ever heard that we're all brothers and sisters down here on earth? I mean, in the end, who is really our father? It's Father in Heaven. I love my family, and I want to be with them, that's true, but there's so much more than that. It's very personal. That's probably why this whole thing with Ben has me so upset. What he sees as a casual, take-it-or-leave-it relationship with God is, in my mind, a very personal and conscious choice—one that has to be taken seriously. He's blowing it off right now, and you have no idea how much that scares me."

"Ah, Ben," Lance said thoughtfully.

"Ah, Ben what?"

"I met Mandy's great-grandmother today," Lance said, knowing he could change the subject, and it would bring on a lot more questions, giving him more time to sit and listen to Enin's voice. He found it comforting and stable.

"Where? How?" Enin asked, shocked.

"At Mandy's old house. Ben went there to pick up some letters and stuff that he had written her over the years."

"Ben went to Mandy's house?" Enin said incredulously.

"Yeah, but that's not the best part. Mandy's great-grandmother, the one who is blind . . ."

"I know who you mean. Go on." Enin asked anxiously.

"She called Ben to repentance, and I swear I thought he was going to go straight to the bishop when we left."

"What?"

"Yeah, it was pretty intense. She says to him that he has to get over Mandy and go on his mission. That he can't continue to use Mandy as his excuse for being inactive. It was pretty spooky. Ben was almost in tears when we left."

"Wow," Enin said, shaking her head. "Wow," she repeated softly.

Lance shrugged. "I thought you would enjoy that." He leaned back on the wall, and she leaned back into him.

"So did he?" Enin said presently.

"What?"

"Go see the bishop?"

"Nah, he downplayed the whole thing when we got back in the truck. He said he was too old to change and put in his Black Sabbath CD."

Enin snorted. "He hates Black Sabbath. That's not even his CD. I think it's Rat's."

Lance nodded. "I noticed he had a pretty extensive

collection of LDS stuff."

"Yeah. He's a funny guy. He talks big, but deep down inside, I think he misses his old life."

"I don't know. All I know is that it was a pretty weird day. Still is actually."

"I know," Enin agreed.

"Mandy's great-grandma said Ben had read the Book of Mormon six times. That kind of blew me away," Lance added as a postscript.

"I know, us too. I mean, I don't know that anyone in our family, except maybe my mom, has read the book that many times."

"So I hate to bring this up, but do you have any suggestions about what to do with Crazy Guy out there?"

"Ooh, I don't want to think about him."

"I know, but as comfy as it is here in this mine shaft, I have a feeling we're going to have to go back to the real world in the morning."

"I know," Enin said. "I'll bet my parents are going crazy right now. I wish I could let them know I'm okay. Do you think the sheriff knows we're missing?" Enin said, stifling a yawn at the same time.

Lance looked at his watch. It was a little past nine. "Yeah, I'm sure of it. They're probably combing these hills right now."

"Why would they be combing the hills looking for us? You didn't know I was here; how would they?"

Lance smiled in the dark. "The same way I did. Most of these guys are Mormon, right? I'm sure they have better access to the Spirit than I do. In fact, I'm still trying to figure out why I'm here."

"I'm not," Enin said as she snuggled under his arm again and laid her head on his chest.

In a few minutes, the only sound that could be heard in the mine was Enin's soft, rhythmic breathing. Lance leaned his head back on the cave wall and slowly shut his eyes.

Wayne slammed his clenched fist down on the steering wheel. He didn't slow down as he passed by the Cooper farm and saw the flashing red lights. Steering with his left hand, he rubbed the top of his head between his beefy thumb and pinky. He was getting one of his headaches again. He leaned over and pull open the empty ashtray, looking for his prescription bottle he had gotten from some free medical clinic in Wendover only a week before. He had to struggle, twisting the small bottle back and forth, to get it past the small metal tab on the ash tray. When it finally popped free, he shook it.

No noise—no pills. He threw the plastic vial on the floor of the Taurus and went back to rubbing his temples. *They should have given me more pills,* he thought.

"She'll have to come with me," he half whispered to the windshield.

"You don't know that!" he shouted in the car. "I'm taking

her anyway . . . No, it's not, and I do know what I am doing . . .
Shut up. Go away!" Wayne said as he started to pound at the
side of his head in a rhythmic pattern with his right fist.

The empty car was the only witness to his momentary
break with reality.

He made a U-turn on Tempo and headed back toward
town.

He sort of needed gas, but every station he passed was
closed. He would get it on his way back to Wendover, after he
picked up the girl.

He increased his speed as he left Magna and headed toward
Hunter.

Leaving the pavement for the gravel road leading to the
campground, he nervously patted the small shoes next to him.
He hoped she hadn't been too uncomfortable. She seemed like
an understanding girl, and it would be nice to have someone
to talk to on the trip back to California.

Rounding the last turn before the campground turnoff,
his headlights caught the back taillights of a truck in the road.
They lit up with the reflection from his Taurus. He chewed
aggressively on his lower lip. He slowed down as he got closer.
It was a dark-colored truck of some kind. There were no other
lights but his own and no sign of people around the truck. He
slowed to a stop behind it.

Getting out of the sedan, he walked around the vehicle.
The ground was muddy, and he could see two sets of large
footprints headed back toward the main road. He looked up
the road toward the campground. This truck had never gotten
that far, and as far as he could tell, neither had the people. He
sighed in relief.

He would have to hurry though; they weren't going to
leave their truck like this in the middle of the road all night.

He reloaded himself in the Taurus and pulled onto the half
gravel, half broken pavement leading to the campground.

The headlights hit the outhouse, and he could see the tape
was still in place. He would just collect the girl and be on his

way. She might have to go in the trunk initially, but he would free her as soon as he collected his stuff in Wendover and was on the road again.

He stifled a yawn with the back of his hand. On second thought, maybe he would just take a short nap first. Maybe it would help with the pain in his temples. There was really no reason the guys in the truck would come to the campground. They would most likely just pick up their truck and be on their way.

Rolling down the window, he listened for any noise the girl might make at his coming. All was quiet. She was probably sleeping. In reality, he knew that people could sleep through anything. There had been many nights in Kuwait when he had curled up next to a set of sandbags and slept as the war whirled around him. It didn't matter how traumatized you were, when you really needed sleep, it would find you.

He slowly rolled his car in front of the outhouse and turned off his engine. He set the alarm on his watch to go off in thirty minutes and found himself asleep in two.

Chapter

19

Sheriff A. J. Lanz closed his cell phone and smiled weakly at his wife, who was watching him from the kitchen door.

"That sounded bad," she said simply as she bounced slightly up and down, comforting an almond-eyed toddler on her hip.

"Maybe. Butler thinks there's been a kidnapping."

"Where?" Melanie Lanz asked.

"Magna," he replied.

"Magna? Seems a bit out of character."

"That's what everyone in Utah seems to think when we have a kidnapping, Magna or otherwise."

"Yeah, I guess you're right. So I guess you won't be home for a while."

"I doubt it. You gonna be okay?"

"I think so. The twins are asleep now. If I can just get this little bug down, we'll be fine. I think the worst is over anyway.

I don't know what else they have to throw up."

"Well, you can always wake up one of the older kids. I'll have the cell. Call if you really need me, though I suspect I'm not going to be much help," he said as he strapped his holster on his chest.

"Girl or boy? Young or old?" Melanie asked.

A.J. sighed. "Girl . . . about nineteen. They think she may have been taken earlier this afternoon."

"Oh, how awful for her. I hope she's okay. I hate this part of your job."

"Me too," A.J. said as he leaned over and kissed his wife.

Pulling out of the driveway in his patrol car, he listened intently to the scanner. There were three cars ahead of him on the way to Magna. Two local deputies, including Butler, were already at the scene.

"A.J. here," he said into the handheld receiver. "What do we have so far?"

Deputy Butler responded, "I've notified the FBI like you asked, and they're on their way. The brother is here with me, but I sent the rest of the family back to their house. We're dusting for prints now."

"You said something about the telephone being disconnected. Have them dust outside near the junction box first. Have you cordoned off the area?"

"Yes, sir."

"All right, my ETA's about five minutes."

A.J. Lanz had been a Salt Lake County sheriff for five years. He came up through the ranks after he had left the marines as an M.P. Most of the time he enjoyed what he did. It didn't get too complicated: catch a few bad guys, take care of mundane personnel issues within the department, go to court and present the law's side of a case.

But the occasional murder or kidnapping did get to him. On one level, he felt kind of like his wife: things like this shouldn't happen in Utah—*land of the Mormons*. But as sad as it was, the practical side of him knew that people were people, LDS or not. It would be foolish to think that all crime committed in Utah emanated from the 40 percent non-LDS population. Good police work depended on objectivity.

A.J. made a right into the driveway. In his headlights, he noted that the name on the mailbox was Cooper. His deputies had set up a few hot, bright halogen lights along the drive, next to the house, and in the back. They cast severe shadows on the ground. On the right, his headlights illuminated a familiar looking raised jeep. He quickly made the mental connection between the name of the kidnapped girl and the young woman he'd given a ticket to the night before.

His black and white Crown Victoria splashed through some large puddles that dotted the drive. Looking toward the eastern sky, he saw that the brunt of the recent storm was heading over the Wasatch Mountains. Each lightning strike that pierced the dark sky silhouetted the jagged range.

Deputy Butler was standing on the porch talking to a young kid. The deputy must have come from a church meeting. He was still in a suit and tie.

Parking on the wet, dead grass of the front lawn, he was careful not to hit the yellow crime scene tape that was festooned from tree to tree and tree to porch railing.

Butler nodded toward A.J.

"Anything new?" A.J. asked as he dipped his six foot four frame under the yellow plastic.

"Not much, A.J. We still have to match prints—but there were some good ones near the phone junction box like you said. There doesn't seem to be anything missing, though clearly the perp was looking for something."

"What about the barn?" A.J. asked.

"Not much there. The kids had cleaned it up before we got here. They didn't know . . ."

"Understood . . ." A.J. cut him off. "Have you considered that this might have been about the former owners, the Coopers?"

"No. Good point. I'll get their current home information," Butler said as he wrote down more notes on his yellow pad.

"And you are?" A.J. reached out a hand toward Ben.

"Ben. Benjamin Woodson." He corrected himself as he shook this tall sheriff's hand. It was a firm, comforting handshake.

"So Ben, what's your take on this?"

"Me?" Ben said.

"Sure," A.J. replied.

"I don't know. This morning I just thought it was some punk kids, but because Enin and Lance are missing—I guess I think it must be connected."

A.J. pulled his brows together. "Lance? I thought the report was that just one person was missing." A.J. looked toward Butler and then back at Ben.

"Lance is our new roommate. He never showed back up. He's the one who wrote the note about Enin being kidnapped. He said he went to get some gun. We assumed he would come back, but it's already eleven o'clock, and he never checked in," Ben said.

"Butler?"

"Well, Sheriff, it's true the kid who wrote the note hasn't come back, but since he wrote the note we didn't figure he'd been kidnapped along with the girl. We're trying to find information about him now.

"Now, Ben, let's you and me talk. Tell me everything that went on today. Start with when you noticed the garage had been broken into."

"I already told this to Bishop . . . I mean, Deputy Butler," Ben said.

"Understood, but I need to hear it firsthand from you."

Ben took a deep breath and began again.

Fifteen minutes later, A.J. flipped his notebook closed and studied Ben.

"So you don't think the gun referred to in the note is the gun he had with him out at the quarry today?"

"I don't think so, but I don't know for sure. I saw him put the broken gun in his pocket."

"Could he have given it to Rat?"

"I don't know. I mean, if he did, I wasn't aware of it. I was with both of them the whole time, well except . . ."

"Except what?" A.J. asked.

"Well, nature called, and I answered . . . but I couldn't have been gone more that a couple of minutes."

"You have a number for this Rat?" A.J. opened up his little book again, in anticipation.

"Yes and no. It's in my cell, and my cell is out of batteries."

"Don't you have a charger somewhere?"

"Yeah, it's in my truck, the truck I asked Lance to bring home—I am assuming he took it to get the gun."

"All right. Let's see if we can get Rat's number some other way."

"Okay," Ben said. "Can I leave now? I told my dad I would report in when I was done."

"Sure," A.J. said, flipping back through his notes, only paying half attention.

"Ah . . . I need a car . . . Can I take my sister's Jeep?" Ben asked, looking toward the Jeep that sat alone in the driveway now.

Enin's phone vibrated in his hand and Ben jumped. He flipped it open. "My folks," he said as he looked at the sheriff. A.J. nodded.

"Give me a few more minutes with the Jeep, okay?" A.J. said quietly as he tucked the little note pad in his shirt pocket. A.J. walked into the house, leaving Ben alone on the porch to answer the phone.

Chapter 20

Enin found herself gradually wakening. She opened her eyes, darkness surrounding her. She tried to comprehend why her head was lying on someone's warm, rhythmically breathing chest. The lub-dub of a strong heartbeat reverberating in her right ear.

Ah, this was Lance. Cali-boy. She was with him because some crazy guy had kidnapped her.

She kept her head where it was and thanked her Heavenly Father for blessings like the Spirit that had whispered to Lance earlier. She wondered at how it all worked, the Spirit and such. Were there spirit helpers who took messages from one spirit to the other, or was Lance's mind opened up to hear her directly?

She had heard of people hearing voices of dead relatives before, but he swore he heard hers, and she was most certainly not dead.

She looked down at Lance's slender arm that had a wristwatch attached. She carefully picked up his arm between her thumb and index finger and tried to catch the time—1 A.M. She was glad he had a digital readout. It was very easy to read in the dark of the cave. His watch cast an eerie green glow on his pant leg. She set his arm back down and wondered if it was one o'clock California or Utah time. Was he the kind of guy who changed his watch immediately—or who adjusted the time in his head in order to avoid the hassle? She somehow expected it was Utah time.

"Can't sleep?" Lance yawned, as he raised his arm to look at his watch.

Enin nervously jumped.

"Sorry, didn't mean to scare you," Lance said.

"No, you didn't scare me. I was just trying to be careful not to wake *you,*" Enin said.

"I was awake already," Lance said.

"You were not," Enin disagreed. "You were sound asleep."

"No, I was awake. I woke up a few minutes ago. I'm probably the one who woke you up. I thought I heard something, but it was probably a bird or something."

"We get hoot owls in our attic sometimes."

"Possibly that. Can you stand being alone for a minute?" Lance asked.

"Uh, not really. Why?" Enin replied hesitantly.

"Nature calls."

"Oh. Actually, nature is calling me too," Enin said, relieved it was only that.

Lance laughed.

"What?" Enin said as she sat up and stretched her arms.

"You were stuck in an outhouse all day. I'm just surprised you have to go at all."

"First, I only used that gross potty once, and second, I drank that Mountain Dew on the way here, remember?"

"Okay. So we'll both go outside," Lance said and stood up.

"Fine," Enin said as she followed him.

Lance pushed opened the iron door. It made a metal-on-metal sound. They both inhaled in unison.

"Do you think anyone heard that?" Enin asked.

"Depends on if anyone is out here listening for weird sounds in the night."

They both stood silent at the entrance to the mine, listening to the dark.

All they heard were a few crickets and random frog sounds. Lance stepped out into the night. Enin held his arm.

"Wait." Enin let go of his arm and turned back into the mine. In the dim light, she retrieved her purse.

"What? You can't go anywhere without your purse?"

"No, I just happen to have some tissues in here."

"Oh," he said, understanding reddening his face.

"I'll go over there," Enin said, pointing to a small out-cropping of boulders.

"Okay, I'll go over here then," he said, pointing in the opposite direction.

When Lance was done, he waited a few minutes before whispering into the night. "Enin?"

"Yeah?" answered her small voice from the semidarkness.

"You done?"

"Yeah. All clear."

Lance walked toward Enin. She was sitting on a flat boulder in front of the overhang.

"You want to go back inside?" Lance asked.

"Not really," she said, pulling her knees up into the body of Ben's sweatshirt to keep them warm.

"Okay," he said.

Enin moved her lunch box so he could sit down beside her. Lance picked up the lunch box.

"So this is a pretty unusual purse."

"I suppose," Enin said, grabbing it from him.

"So what do girls keep in those things anyway?" he asked.

"Lots of stuff."

"Like what?" Lance insisted.

"Oh, the same kind of stuff you have in your wallet."

"I doubt it," Lance said.

"What? You've never seen in a girl's purse?"

"Not really," he admitted.

"You have sisters, don't you?"

"Sure, but I've never gone through their purses. I don't think I would have wanted to actually."

"But you want to go through mine?" Enin said.

"Uh . . . yeah."

"Why?" Enin asked, puzzled.

Lance shrugged. "I don't know. It just seems interesting. You're not a normal girl. I figure your purse would be an extension of that."

Enin frowned. "Oh thanks. Not normal, huh? I have to tell you, lines like that are not winning you points."

"What? That you're not like a normal girl? You aren't. I can't be the first one to point that out," Lance said with complete innocence.

Enin turned her head, "No, you're not, Lance," she said, her voice cracking.

"Oh shoot. You're not crying are you?"

"No," Enin lied.

"Hey, I didn't mean to upset you. I like different. I find you very interesting. You're not exactly like the other girls in my ward. I really like that."

"Hmph!" Enin said skeptically, wiping at her nose with a clean tissue. "Most people don't. Especially guys."

"Well, Enin, you may have noticed sometime in the past few days, I'm not like most guys."

"I don't know about that. In a lot of ways you are. You like cars, you're slightly rebellious, you're chauvinistic . . ."

"Chauvinistic? I don't think so. I think I treat girls pretty well."

"It's not that. You just don't think we can do stuff as well as you. Like the transmission help I offered, you didn't take me seriously, did you?"

"Well . . ."

"I rest my case," Enin said and wrapped her arms around her legs to keep the cold at bay.

"Okay, I concede that point at least. It is a bit out of the ordinary for most girls to know about cars."

"Not if your dad's a mechanic and you work in his shop," Enin said.

"What else do you do that I don't know about?"

Enin shrugged. "I don't know. I like to work on cars. I don't really like to do domestic stuff."

"But you come and make dinner for your brother and his friends all the time."

"Cooking is okay, I guess. I don't like the cleanup part."

"Who does?" Lance agreed. "But that's normal. See, you're pretty normal after all."

Enin narrowed her eyes at him.

"Sorry. So what else?" Lance continued.

"I like the gospel."

"Not so unusual for Utah, Enin. Lots of people around here like the Church," Lance said.

"Ah, you weren't listening, Lance. I said I liked the gospel, not the Church."

"So . . . what?" Lance asked, slightly confused. "You don't like the Church?"

"No. I didn't say that . . . okay, clearly I'm not communicating with you. I like the gospel. I like the way the whole big picture fits together. I like how I feel peace when I read the scriptures. I like it that when I pray, I'm overcome with gratitude for living in the world I do—which includes my family and friends. I love how the whole thing fits together and makes perfect sense."

Lance leaned back, his hands tripodding behind him supporting the weight of his body. He looked up at the sky. He didn't reply.

Enin gave Lance the gift of silence, something not all girls are capable of. She sat next to him as he watched the heavens.

Presently, Lance took in a deep breath, and exhaled.

"Okay, I envy that," he said.

"That's good," Enin whispered softly.

"What? Envy? I thought it was one of the deadly sins or something."

"Depends on what you envy, or in this case, covet. The words are pretty interchangeable, and to covet just means you want something that you don't have. You see something else good that someone has and you would like it for yourself. Do you have that little flashlight?"

"Yeah." He pulled it out of a pocket and handed it to her.

She opened up her lunch box and pulled out two small maroon books.

"You keep books in your purse?" he asked, mildly surprised.

"Not just any books." She handed them to him and turned on the light.

In the bright puddle of light he could see she had a diminutive Bible and Book of Mormon in her hands. "Scriptures?" Lance said, surprised.

"Sure, you know what they say: 'Don't leave home with out them.'" Enin smiled back.

"I think they're referring to some credit card when they say that."

"Well, it applies here too." She took back the Bible and started flipping through it. Then she cleared her voice and read, "'But covet earnestly the best gifts.' That's from 1st Corinthians." Enin shut the little book and continued. "What you say you envy, you can have. You're supposed to covet righteousness. I think if people gave it much thought they would agree that an awful lot of life on earth is spent coveting what others have, including the really good stuff, like happy families, peace, and financial freedom."

"Mmm. . ." Lance responded and then he said, "Well, as

my stepdad used to say, 'Wantin' and gettin' are two separate things.'"

"Well, no offense to your stepdad, but he's wrong. You can't 'get' unless you 'want' first. So one leads to the other," Enin said.

"Okay, point taken." Lance shifted the weight of his body and sat up straighter. He leaned forward and wrapped his arms around his legs—not so much from the cold as from the tiny fire he could feel burning in his stomach. After a moment of quiet between them, he asked. "So how'd you get so smart, Enin?"

Enin shrugged her shoulders. "I don't know. Part 'inspiration'—I read the scriptures daily, and part 'perspiration'—I work at applying them. It's not a hard formula, Lance. You could have what I have too. So could Ben, but you both have to want it."

"I can't speak for Ben, you're probably right about him, but I'm not so sure about me, Enin. You make it sound pretty easy, and from my experience it's not. I read the scriptures. I read the Book of Mormon. I'm not feeling the love here, you know what I mean?"

"No, I don't, because I am clearly feeling the 'love' here, or at least the 'spirit'—same thing, you know. I'm sitting right next to you, Lance. You can't be so dense that you can't feel it too."

Lance didn't respond. He *was* feeling "it." The "it" he hadn't felt in such a long time, and he was scared. He rubbed at his chest and could feel the rapid beating of his heart. He let his hands fall on his lap. His breathing was fully oxygenating his racing mind. It didn't help when the next minute he found Enin's hand on his. He pulled his hand away from under hers.

Enin slowly started to draw her hand back, but before she did, Lance reached out and took it. He moved it toward his lips and kissed the back of it.

Chapter

21

Using the spare keys under the seat, Ben started up Enin's Jeep. It was a little after midnight, and Sheriff Lanz had finally released her car to their family. There was still a fine powdery substance over much of the vehicle from the dusting for prints. The gas gauge registered full. *So like Enin,* he thought, *to keep the tank topped off.*

The past six hours of his life had taken on a surreal quality. He'd helped the sheriff's department determine what might or might not have been taken. It was clear that nothing of value was gone. Among the three—now four—roommates, they had quite an extensive stereo system. It alone was worth thousands. It had not been touched.

A.J. had asked him a ton of questions about Enin, which he could mostly answer, and a ton more questions about Lance, which he could not.

All he could say about Lance was that he had a sense that

he was an all right guy. There was absolutely nothing that would lead him to believe he might have been involved, but he had to admit to himself and the sheriff that he had only known Lance for two days, so he supposed he could have been fooled by him.

When the sheriff asked why Lance had left his family in California, Ben had to acknowledge he didn't know. In fact, everything Lance had ever said about his former life was now taking on new meaning when seen through the law's eyes. Even so, Ben didn't feel anxious about Lance. He had a deep-down feeling that Lance was on their side and that he wasn't the creep who broke in.

His dad had called him on Enin's phone while he was waiting for the Jeep to be released. Both his uncle and his parents' bishop were at the family home. Many of his brothers and some of his sisters-in-law were also there, depending on who could get a sitter at this late hour. His dad mentioned that his mother had asked for a blessing, which was given; then she took a sedative and was now sleeping fitfully on the couch.

Ben had told his dad he didn't know when he could get away but that when he did he would come home. But as he sat in the driveway, listening to the finely tuned engine purr, he had another thought.

He pulled out and headed south toward Rat's house.

Rat lived on the outskirts of Hunter. If people judged where you lived by how you looked, they would have Rat living in a trailer park. He was scruffy, edgy, and full of attitude. He was pierced, tattooed, and occasionally mohawked.

Ben slowly turned right onto the drive that lead to Rat's house. He had to stop and punch in the code to get past the security gates. He drove slowly down the quarter-mile stamped concrete driveway that led to Rat's apartment, which was above the multicar garage and to the side of the 10,000 square foot home his parents lived in. This was no trailer park.

Rat almost always left his truck out. He could have used one of the eight garages if he wanted, but he didn't like taking the time to pull his truck in and out. When he wanted to leave, he wanted to leave.

Unfortunately, Rat's truck was nowhere to be seen. Ben doubted if he was home. The lights of his apartment were dark. Most people might assume that Rat was just asleep, but Rat was a night owl. If his lights were out at midnight, it just meant he wasn't home yet, not that he was in bed. If he was home, even if he was sleeping, his lights were on. No, Ben sighed heavily, he knew Rat was still out. He pulled into the circular driveway in front of the main house and headed back toward the road. He tapped his fingers nervously on the steering wheel of the Jeep. He was wide awake, probably from adrenalin, and didn't want to go home yet, but he didn't know what else to do. He waited while the black metal gate slowly opened for him to leave the grounds. Then he headed back toward the main road. When he got to the highway, he started to make the right turn toward home but changed his mind so suddenly that he made the Jeep's big tires squeal in protest. He turned left instead.

Lance had said something about getting the gun. Maybe it had dropped out of his pocket or something when they were leaving the quarry; they were running pretty fast because of the rain. The Jeep was picking up speed as he headed south. The storm was off in the distance and in its wake were a hundred million stars that punched through the night sky. The moon was big, yellow, and full. He felt a gradual peace settle over him for the first time that evening. He was headed in the right direction.

When he turned onto the gravel road, his headlights caught the silhouette of a truck he would know anywhere—his.

Chapter

22

A.J. watched from the front window as Ben pulled out of the driveway and then turned to the assembled group of sheriffs in front of him who were quietly talking among themselves. "Butler, I want at least two of your men stationed here in case either of the kids return. Except for the lieutenant, the rest of you can go back to the station."

An older black deputy raised his hand, which A.J. acknowledged with a nod.

"What about the media?"

"They'll probably be at the station when you get there. Set up a press conference for 6 A.M. so we can get something on the morning news. I'll be back by then," A.J. said.

"Are you going to be here?" the deputy asked.

"Yes, for a while, but I have to go home and check on my family sometime tonight also; a couple of the kids have been pretty sick."

"Your kids or the adopted ones?" a newer deputy asked.

The muffled voices in the crowd immediately went silent, and all heads turned toward Sheriff Lanz. A.J. had his lower lip firmly between his teeth, his eyes turned toward the ceiling, and his face pinched and drawn. He took a deep breath and then exhaled evenly before he spoke.

"They are *all* my kids, the black ones too, okay?" A.J. said with a metered voice.

"Uh, sure. Sorry. No offense intended." The deputy took a step back, deeper into the safety of the crowd.

A.J. turned and walked out to the front porch. He shut the door a bit too solidly, and the whole house shook. He flipped open his phone and called home. His wife answered on the first ring.

"Everything okay, A.J.?" she said quietly.

"Yeah. It's going as well as can be expected. I kind of thought you'd be asleep."

A soft laugh came from the other end of the phone. "Then why'd you call?"

He sighed.

"What's the matter, A.J.? This isn't about the case is it?"

He didn't reply for a moment and shook his head as if his wife could see him.

"A.J.?"

"Yeah, I'm here."

"What's the matter?"

"You know what I hate?" he continued without letting his wife respond. "I hate having to explain every darn day about why we adopted kids. I hate it that there is some sort of perception that we are either 'saints' or 'wackos' for adopting kids from other races. I hate the looks I get from the black guys in the unit—like I'm taking the kids away from them somehow. Yet, I don't see them adopting the kids—only whispering about it behind my back."

"Obviously someone said something about it tonight," his wife observed.

A.J. leaned his head up against the rail. He could see the moon over the mountains from his position. "Not directly, just asked if 'my' kids or the adopted ones were sick. It was an honest question, I suppose, but I try so hard not to differentiate between them."

"A.J.," his wife said softly, "they are different. They are totally ours for eternity, but they *are* different. We have two beautiful little black boys and two gorgeous Korean daughters. They are a wonderful addition to our two biological children—but they are always going to be black and Korean. Our grandchildren from them will never have red hair like you, or green eyes like me. They aren't going to morph into our blood lines as they reach adulthood."

"I know, but . . ." A.J.'s voice trailed off.

"This is really about "him," isn't it?" his wife said gently.

"I had another dream."

"When?" His wife's voice rose in concern.

"Last night."

"Why didn't you tell me?"

A.J. shrugged. "I don't know."

"Well?"

"Same old dream. He's trapped in a dark space and is calling me. I try to reach him, but the darkness is overwhelming. I reach out and touch his fingers, but that's all I can feel."

"A.J. It wasn't your fault. You didn't do anything."

A.J. slammed his fist on the rail. "That's just it, Melanie, I didn't do anything. I didn't even try. And it *was* my fault. I knew he was in trouble. I should have left as soon as I heard, but I didn't. I was . . . too embarrassed, or ashamed, or weak. I didn't do anything, and I have paid for it ever since."

"The bishop said you have to let it go."

"I would love to. Do you think I like these dreams? Do you think I don't pray every night that I can sleep just one night in peace?"

"You don't even know it was a he anyway," Melanie said.

A.J. sighed again. "It was. I know. I know as much as I

know anything in my life. It was a he. He needed me and I failed him."

"Well, we need you too, A.J. The kids you have now need you."

"I know, and I love you and the kids. I really do. I treasure our time together. I just can't help but wonder if I will ever meet him on the other side. And if I did, would he hate me?" He didn't wait for his wife to answer. "Of course he would."

"A.J., let it go, please," his wife said, ever so softly.

"Honey, I've got to get back to work. Thanks for letting me vent. I'll be okay. I doubt if I'll be home tonight. If I can, I'll catch a few winks at the station, but we've called a press conference for six o'clock, so if you want to see much of me the next few days just watch the news."

"I love you, A.J."

"And I love you back," A.J. said and pressed "end" as the front door opened and Deputy Butler stepped out.

"The 4Runner in the garage is registered to a Joseph Raintree in California. We're trying to locate him now," the deputy said.

A.J. opened his mouth to speak but his cell phone rang. He put a finger in the air, signaling Deputy Butler to wait while he took the call. He flipped the phone open and put it to his ear.

"Sheriff Lanz?" a voice asked breathlessly.

"Yes."

"This is Ben. I found my Blazer. It's out near where we where shooting, but it's locked, and Lance isn't here."

Chapter

23

"Where are you exactly?" A.J. asked.

Ben shifted in the seat of the still-running Jeep. Turning slightly, he could see the campground sign in the light that spilled over from his headlamps. "I'm where the road forks near Lone Oak Campground."

"Okay, we're on our way. Stay on the phone with me."

"No problem . . . wait . . . I think I see someone. There's someone at the top of the hill. Hold on." Ben put the phone down on his lap and cupped his hands around his mouth. "Hey, you seen any kids around here? A young girl and a boy maybe."

For an answer, he saw a bright flash of blue light. It momentarily silhouetted a man with a rifle. He heard the crack of the gun. Immediately to his right a shot ricocheted off the roll bar.

"Snap!" Ben yelled as he shoved the Jeep into reverse. The

cell phone on his leg went bouncing to the floor, and he spun up a tangle of wet rock that pelleted his parked Blazer as he backed down the wet road in Enin's Jeep.

Another crack and a bullet hit, penetrating the Jeep's windshield on the passenger side. The glass shattered but held together. *Boy is Enin going to be mad,* Ben thought. This guy meant business.

He could vaguely hear Sheriff Lanz's voice coming from his phone, but this wasn't a good time to talk.

Another shot. Another blow to the windshield. Another hole—this time closer to where he was seated. Maybe backing up with his headlights acting as targets wasn't such a good idea.

Ben started to turn the wheel clockwise to change directions, but his back right wheel dipped down in the smallish gully made by the recent rains. Enin's Jeep bounced sideways and some of the glass in the windshield fell forward onto the hood. A small flap of glass remained intact at the top of the metal frame, momentarily held in place by four inches of adhesive sunshield. Ben jammed the car into first and turned the wheels tight and to the left, the second grating bounce releasing the rest of the glass.

The fourth shot hit his left arm before exiting through the open air windshield.

"Double snap!" Ben said in astonishment. He had actually been shot, and it hurt like nothing else. The burning sensation ran up and down his left arm. He knew he was bleeding because the wind blasting him from the front was cold where the blood was running.

He didn't stop though. He pushed through the gears with his left arm even though his fingers were weak and starting to tingle. He was running on pure adrenalin. He was back on the old gravel road and into third gear by the time he heard the fifth shot, which thankfully missed him.

He spun his tires as he made a jarring sharp right on the highway and pulled out onto the open road. He figured his heart was taching at about five thousand rpm. Any faster and he was sure he was going to redline and have a full-blown heart attack.

He knew he was in fight or flight mode and he was taking flight. He was doing almost ninety mph as he sped down the highway toward Hunter. He didn't pull over until he was back in the small town. By that time, he could see the flashing lights up ahead. He knew he could stop now, so he pulled into the closed convenience store he and Lance had been at earlier that day. He pushed the gearshift into first and reached up for the first time to feel where he'd been hit.

He felt the wet rip in his shirt and thought of Enin. She'd bought him this shirt last month for his twenty-third birthday. Ben wondered if she was going to be as mad as he was that his shirt was toast.

Three sheriff's cars pulled into the store almost simultaneously. Sheriff Lanz was the first one at his side.

"My gosh, Ben, have you been shot?" He turned to a deputy. "Get an ambulance here, *now!*" Turning back to Ben, he said, "What happened?"

Ben started to shrug and then winced from the pain. "I don't know. I went back to where we were shooting this afternoon to see if maybe Lance had gone back there, and I saw my truck. Then I see this guy, and he starts shooting at me. I got out as quick as I could."

"Butler! Bring me the first aid kit. This kid is losing too much blood. Where's that ambulance?"

Deputy Butler was already running toward the Jeep with the kit. "It's about five minutes out."

"Okay," A.J. said, though it didn't sound like it was okay to Ben.

"Ben? I want to get you out of this Jeep. Can you help?"

"Uh, sure," Ben said. He unlatched his belt with his right hand and put his left foot over the side. A moment later he crumpled into A.J.'s arms in a dead faint.

Chapter

24

Enin felt a little shudder run up her spine as Lance's lips brushed the back of her hand; then she twitched as she heard the first "crack" in the distance.

"What was that?" Enin said, not really wanting to know.

Lance jumped off the flat rock they were sitting on and turned his right ear toward the sound in the distance when they both heard the second shot from the gun.

"Back inside the cave," he whispered loudly to Enin.

"Not without you," Enin replied, her voice quivering.

"I'm right behind you, believe me."

Enin grabbed her scriptures and shoved them in her purse and latched it. She knocked the flashlight off the rock, and it bounced on the ground. Lance reached down and picked it up.

"Keep this off and come on," he said, his voice tight.

"I am. I am."

The third shot found Enin stumbling forward over Ben's oversized shoes as she tripped on a loose rock near the cave entrance.

"Who's he shooting at?" Enin said.

"I don't want to think about it right now. Get in the cave. How far back does it go?"

"I'm not sure. I've only been in here a few times with Ben and his friends. We didn't go that far in," she replied.

"Well, we're about to find out," Lance said as he plunged toward the back of the cave.

"What about the flashlight?" Enin asked, her voice edging toward terror.

"You can turn it on now. I was only trying to keep us in the dark outside. The shots are too far away for him to be close, but I didn't want to take any chances. I honestly don't know who's shooting at what right now."

From the mouth of the cave, they heard another shot, but this one was muffled by the cave.

"That's four," Enin cried.

"Our job is to not be around when he gets to five," Lance said as he pressed deeper in the cave, the small intense light casting harsh shadows across the loose, jagged rocks on the ground ahead of them both.

For an answer, shot number five could be heard, but with much less punch.

"Who's he shooting at?" Enin said again.

"How do you know it's even him who's doing the shooting? Maybe it's the police. Maybe they're shooting back. Maybe there are lots of people out there."

"It sounded like the same gun," Enin said.

"Can you really tell the difference?" Lance replied as he tripped but then caught himself on the cave wall.

"I could this afternoon. I couldn't tell what you were shooting, but I could tell you had different guns—including something automatic," Enin said as she grabbed the belt loop on the back of Lance's pants. She was trying to keep up, but he was going a little too fast for her. He felt the immediate pressure of his jeans being tugged at. Lance slowed down, but Enin didn't remove her two fingers from his belt loop.

Up ahead, the light left the ground as it illuminated a large opening in the ground. Lance stopped, and Enin ran into the back of him.

"What's this?" Lance said as he turned the light into a massive hole in the rock floor. The opening was man-made and ran at an angle deep into the earth. Along one side was a series of decaying planks that had served as makeshift steps to descend into the bowels of the mine.

"What kind of mine was this anyway?" Lance asked.

"I don't know," Enin said. "I know they have copper mines around here."

"I thought they mined copper in open pits," Lance said.

Enin shrugged. "Yeah, but can't they get it this way too?"

"I don't know. Did they mine for silver or gold here?"

"Silver, maybe, but gold no. At least I think I would have heard about gold mining in Utah if they had."

Lance moved the beam of light around the area. There was part of an old wooden bench along the side of the wall with a few soda cans tossed under it. As the light circled the walls of the cave, they could both see a fair amount of graffiti in both English and Spanish.

"Equal opportunity taggers," Lance said as he read the various mild to obscene writings on the rocks. There was only one way into this room of the mine: the way they had come. If they wanted to leave, they had to either go back or go down.

"Do you want to stay here?" Lance said to Enin, who was still holding on to him by his jeans.

"As opposed to what?"

"Going down, I guess," Lance said.

"There?" Enin's voice rose an octave.

"Look, we can go down, stay here, or go back. Do you have an opinion?"

"Uh, I don't like any of those choices," Enin said.

"Then I say we go down. I suspect this shaft leads to another room or series of tunnels. If you look down it, you can see that the taggers have been at work in it too. So it's probably safe enough." Lance reached behind him and gently unhooked Enin's fingers from his belt loop. He took her hand in his and moved her closer to the edge of the downward-sloping tunnel.

"You're going to need both hands though. You'll probably have to leave the lunch box," Lance said.

"Bad idea, Lance. If he does come in here, he'll know which way we went. Maybe we could run your belt through the handle," Enin suggested.

"Yeah, that would work," Lance said as he let go of Enin's hand to unlatch his buckle. He pulled his belt out halfway and inserted it into the black plastic handle of the metal box. When he latched his belt back up, the box dangled over his rear.

"I think we need to crawl down backward. It's too steep for us to keep our balance and just walk down these boards. Also, we can use our hands to steady ourselves as we go. I'll go first and you follow me."

"Okay," Enin said.

"I think the shooting has stopped—for now at least."

"Maybe he's reloading."

"Well, that's positive thinking," Lance said, but his voice had the slightest hint of a chuckle as he turned around and started down the steep slope.

"Are you laughing at me?" Enin said incredulously.

"Laughing with you, Enin. Laughing with you."

"I wasn't laughing, Lance," Enin said as she followed his lead.

The flashlight illuminated the roof instead of the dark shaft since they were going in feet first. Lance put a little weight on each plank and bounced to make sure it could hold his entire weight before he moved down a level.

On about the twentieth plank, the soft, rotting wood

broke in half, and Lance slipped down a plank. Losing his balance, he grabbed for the plank above him with both hands and let go of the flashlight, which went tumbling down the interior tunnel of the earth. The light bounced crazily off the wall—then ceiling—then wall of the shaft. The flashlight fell deeper into the mine. Halfway down, the bouncing caused the light to cease, leaving only the metal pinging sounds of the flashlight hitting the planks—then rocks—then planks as it tumbled freely.

Then the cave was silent once more, except for the rapid breathing of Lance and Enin.

"You okay?" Lance asked Enin.

"Me? You're the one who fell. Are you okay?"

"Yeah, I'm fine," Lance said. Then he went on. "Well, as fine as I can be for an idiot who just dropped our only light."

"What now?" Enin asked.

"Keep going, I guess. I'm hoping we can find the flashlight when we get to the bottom."

"How far is that?" Enin said.

"Don't know, but I know there is one, because the flashlight stopped. Enin, be really careful on the next step—sort of straddle it. It broke in the middle but seems to be attached on either side. I'm going to start putting my weight on the sides from now on. They seem more stable."

"Okay," Enin said as she felt her way down the next step. She jumped slightly when she felt Lance's hand on her calf.

"Sorry, I didn't mean to startle you. I just wanted you to know I was here."

"No, I appreciate it. Really," Enin said.

Step by step, they descended the inky shaft.

"One hundred and seventy-two," Lance said.

"What?"

"Planks. One hundred and seventy-two planks. I'm at the bottom. You're almost here. I'm going to reach out and touch you again, so don't scream." He reached out his arms and touched the back of Enin's legs, gently guiding them toward the ground.

"What about the flashlight?" Enin said.

"I'm going to look for it right now. You stand there for a minute, okay?"

"Yeah."

Lance knelt down and patted the ground.

"Hey, wait. I have a book of matches in my purse," Enin said.

Lance stood up. "Why does that not surprise me?" He very slowly tapped his feet on the ground to feel his way back to Enin's side.

Enin had her arms out, rotating in front of her to feel him coming closer. He bumped into one of her hands with his chest. He reached out, took her arm, and then moved toward her, wrapping both of his around her. She gasped slightly and then put her arms around him so tightly he could hardly breathe. She began to shake and cry at the same time.

"It's okay," he said as he ever so gently stroked the top of her head.

"This is the worst day of my life," Enin said. Lance could feel hot tears on the side of his neck.

"This is probably the weirdest day of my life," Lance replied.

Enin sniffed, "Not the worst?"

"Nah, not the worst," Lance said.

"So when was the worst?"

"Probably the day my mom died."

"I thought you said you were really little."

"I was, but I still remember the day she died."

"I'm so sorry, Lance. It must have been horrible."

"It was. Do you believe I still miss her? I mean, I only knew her for six years, but I still miss her."

"What do you miss about her most—if you don't mind my asking?"

"No. I guess I don't mind. I don't talk about her much, not because it's painful really. I just don't have anyone to talk with about her. My brother and sister don't remember her at all. I think I miss her smell."

"Her smell?"

"Yeah. She used to wear this green perfume, Emerald, or something like that."

"Emeraude?"

"Yeah. How'd you know?"

"I have some, but it's hard to find. My grandmother used to wear it, and I would sneak into hers. It's in a green bottle."

"Yeah. I still have the bottle," Lance said.

"You mean back at your house in California? You kept it all this time?"

"Actually, it's at Blake's. I packed it when I left. It's one of the only things I have of my mother's. That, a picture, and a letter she wrote."

"Oh, wow."

"Hey, can you get in your purse now?" Lance asked.

"Sure, turn around."

Lance let go of Enin and turned. Enin carefully made sure her lunch box wouldn't drop its contents when she opened it; then she unlatched it and felt around for the box of waterproof matches. Latching it back up, she patted Lance on the shoulder for him to turn around. She moved her fingers down his arm until she found his hand and placed the matches in them.

"Thanks," Lance said. "I'm going to light one, and we'll see if we can find that darn flashlight."

He only fumbled slightly as he lit the match and then handed the box back to her. The match flared up for a second, lighting the entire lower level of the cave. They could both see the flashlight against the far wall.

"Stay here," Lance said as he held the match out in front of him and walked toward the flashlight. He bent down and picked it up; then he shook out the match as he tried to turn the flashlight on. The flashlight wasn't cooperating. He shook it, and a faint light glowed from the bulb and then faded to black again.

"Is it broken?" Enin asked.

"Yeah, I think so, but let me work with it a sec," Lance

said, as he concentrated on the flashlight.

Enin could hear him shaking the light, and then the light went on and filled the cavern with light. Lance walked back toward her, Enin's metal purse bouncing on his hip.

"The cap was loose; that's all. I think it's okay now, but we shouldn't keep it on."

"I know," Enin said with sadness.

"Look, we can use it to find somewhere to sit and then turn it off. We'll wait for a while and then go back up, okay?"

Enin nodded her head.

Lance moved the light around each wall. There were two tunneled hallways that left the room: one to the right, one to the left.

"Which one?" Lance said to Enin as he moved the light back and forth between the two.

"Oh, I always 'choose the right,' of course," Enin smiled.

"Funny," he laughed.

"Hey, I try," Enin giggled, her laughter tickling the top of the cavern.

"I'm going to take this lunch box off now," Lance said as he undid his belt buckle and slipped the handle off.

Enin took her purse and wrapped her arms tightly around it. She shuddered, the contents rattling next to her chest.

"Cold?" Lance asked.

"A little," she responded.

"You probably need to move a little more. Jump up and down and stuff." As he said this, Lance began to jump from foot to foot. Then he started hopping like a rabbit.

"Is this how you impressed the girls at the dances?" Enin said, shaking her head.

On Lance's third bunny hop, the floor of the cave gave way, and Lance slipped into the bowels of the earth, twisting awkwardly to the rhythm of Enin's primal screams.

Enin jumped away from the widening hole in the ground and continued her panicked cries. Dust and grit puffed up out of the hole, filling the cavern with choking debris.

Chapter
25

Wayne stood on the top of the small rise by the campground and watched as the 4x4 turned onto the highway. Because the girl was still in the outhouse, when nature had called he had headed this way just in time to see a vehicle careening up the gravel road. It had only taken him seconds to get his rifle out of the trunk before the kid had headed toward the campground. He stood looking at the remaining Blazer, wondering if he should go down and check it out more closely or just go get the girl and leave now. He tensed and then shuddered violently in response to another stabbing pain in his right temple. Raising his gun, he hit the side of his head with the butt in an effort to stop the cattle-prod feel of the twinge.

He turned, decision made, and walked back toward the Taurus. He had to leave quickly now. No doubt the idiot in the 4x4 would call the police. Unfortunately, his aim had been way off. He had wanted to pop the tires to slow him down, not shoot out the windshield. He tapped the gun butt rhythmically against the side of his head as he made his way up the slight incline.

"Hey, pretty girl!" he yelled as he approached the outhouse. "Wake up. We have to leave now. No more beauty sleep for you."

He walked around the back of his car to get to the outhouse and began looking for the edge of the duct tape. Twelve inches of tape was hanging limply down the left side of the portable commode. Wayne frowned and then grimaced against another sharp head pain.

"What the . . ?" he said, pulling at the tape. It freely moved away from the outhouse. In some places, it wasn't even adhering anymore. He ran around the outhouse twice, unbinding what had already been unbound earlier and then replaced.

Yanking the creaking door open, he was not surprised to find the outhouse empty. "Ow," he said, closing his eyes momentarily in response to the searing pain; he needed his pills. He could see moonlight through the gaping hole in the roof of the outhouse. If he wasn't in such a hurry, and if his head wasn't killing him, he would almost be impressed with the girl's clever breakout.

He slammed the door shut, but the force just caused it to bounce back open. He shut it more slowly the second time and hurriedly got in the Taurus.

Scooting his body into the driver's seat, he saw the little pair of shoes he had taken with him earlier. He picked them up and threw them violently out the door before he shut it. He had to think, but he was having a difficult time between the rapidly increasing contractions in the side of his head. He laid his forehead on the top of the steering wheel as he turned the key. The car sprang to life.

He slowly pulled his head up and squinted through the glass as he put the car in gear and moved forward without headlights—just in case. He was not going to stop and look for the girl, that much was certain. He didn't have the time, and he certainly didn't have the energy. She was on her own. Even more frustrating was that he would now have to abandon his search for the gun. Hopefully, he could get a few hours' start toward California before she or the kid in the Jeep got to anyone.

Leaving the barren campground, he slowly passed the Blazer on his way out to the main road. He stopped briefly to pound on the side of his head again. Using a small penlight, he looked at his map. He wasn't going to risk going through Magna again. He would head south and connect up with 71 West. Heading back to California on I-15 was a safer bet.

He was a few miles down the darkened road when he saw flashing lights in his rearview mirror, but he figured they were too far away to see him now. He was glad his lights were still off. He could actually see fairly well in the light of the full moon. He gradually increased his speed until he was cruising at over ninety-five miles per hour.

He never saw the deer, but the impact shattered the front window, sending beads of glass and tufts of blood-soaked fur into the car. After that, all he really knew was that the pain in his head was gone.

Chapter

26

Jamming her fist in her mouth, Enin was able to stop screaming for a moment. The sound of miniature rocks skittering down below her and the throbbing of the blood in her ears was all she heard at first. Then she heard the faintest of groans. Muffled, the piteous sound drew her to her knees, despite the danger. She lay prostrate on the ground, and inched her way toward the hole. She tentatively crawled toward the edge and put her chin over the open wound in the earth.

"Lance?"

The sound of rocks grating against other and small pebbles falling toward a hellish abyss was the only answer.

"Lance? Oh, please, Lance, you have to answer me."

Nothing.

Eyes closed, Enin prayed. A prayer of anguish and fear. She wondered if she had the faith to pull off a miracle—because she knew nothing but a miracle was going to save them now.

Suddenly, out of the darkness, a light flickered from below, the light hazy and muffled in dust.

"Lance!" she fairly screamed in the gaping hole.

A low moan in the darkness was her only answer, but to her ears it was a sweet moan—a moan only someone alive could make. She would take it.

"Lance, if you can hear me, maybe you can move the flashlight."

The light undulated between the rocks, blocking her view.

Enin sighed and bit the end of her lip. It was a start.

"Lance, listen, don't try to talk. I don't even know if you can, but if you can move the flashlight, we can still communicate. I'm going to ask you some questions. If the answer is yes, wiggle the flashlight; if no, don't wiggle the flashlight. Okay?

Shadows moved back and forth below her.

"Okay. Are you hurt?"

Dancing shadows.

"Is it your head?"

More dancing beams of light.

"What about your body?"

Light flickered below.

"Do you think anything is broken?"

Ribbons of light cut through the pile of rubble.

"An arm?"

The stillness of the light responded.

"Okay, your arms are okay. Well, I suppose that is relatively speaking. How about your leg, or legs?"

The light flickered again.

"But you can't speak?"

Again the light moved.

"Did you hurt your mouth, or teeth, or something?"

The light was still.

"I don't understand. Why can't you talk?"

Nothing.

"Oh, I'm sorry, that was dumb. Wrong kind of question.

Are you, like, pinned by a rock somehow so that you can't talk?"

The light moved in a rapid fashion.

"Oh, Lance, I'm so sorry. You can breathe, though, right?"

The glow below her moved ever so slightly.

"Okay, I'm going to go for help, crazy man or not. Maybe you were right, and the police are up there now. Either way, I'm going."

The light flickered back and forth again.

"I still have the matches, so maybe I can make a fire out of some stuff in my purse. Then I could at least see my way back to the main level."

Lance moved his light in approval.

"Hold on," Enin said. Backing up on her knees until her feet touched the side of the cavern, she dragged her purse behind her.

The cave was ever so dimly lit from Lance's flashlight below. Only because she had been in the dark so long was it enough light for her to rummage through her purse.

She dumped the contents on the cold, gravelly floor, looking for things that would burn.

She had two books of scripture, her checkbook and register, and possibly the checkbook cover itself, though that might only melt. She opened her wallet next and started pulling out pictures, old movie receipts, and notes from friends. She also had a small plastic case of unmentionable feminine supplies. Last, but not least, she had a teddy bear-shaped bottle of rose-colored fingernail polish. She supposed that could act as an accelerant.

"Lance." She raised her voice slightly since she was not directly over the hole in the ground. "Can you hear me?"

She could see the light ever so slightly moving in the hole.

"Good. I have some stuff here that I think I could start a small fire with. I thought I could start the fire sort of near the bottom of the shaft we came down, and that would light my way as I went up. Then when I got into the other cave I could use the matches one at a time to get to the cave entrance. Do you think that would be okay? I mean, you don't think that would make too much smoke for you in the cave, do you?"

No light movement.

"Oh, too many questions and too open-ended, right?"

The shadows danced gracefully on the cavern ceiling. The dust was settling, letting more light through.

"Do you think this is a good plan?"

Dancing shadows again.

"One more question. I think I should lay the things I have to burn in a row, rather than in pile. Do you think they would burn longer that way?"

Lance moved his light.

"Okay, we have a plan. I'm going to start the fire and climb out as quickly as I can. I think you should turn off your light until you hear me coming back for you. I promise I *will* return, Lance." Enin leaned over her little pile and began arranging them like a string of dominoes so as one item finished burning it would catch the other one on fire.

As she put the last item down carefully, she said into the semidarkness, "Lance, you're a good person. I'm sorry if I didn't see that in the beginning. You can be Ben's friend forever—okay? And one more thing, you have to pray for me while I'm gone. Will you do that?"

The light gently bounced off the rocks below, tiny fingers of light caressing the cavern ceiling.

Enin sucked on her lower lip as she lit the first match. Much to her surprise, the fire started on the first try. She quickly stood up and reached for the bottom two-by-four rung that was the first step out.

Following Lance's advice, she kept her feet toward the outside of the rungs and climbed up as fast as she could. She could smell the smoke below her and felt rather like Santa Claus must while ascending through a chimney. The fire was bright below her, revealing the spray-painted marks of many before her. She wondered what type of person would bother to stop on this shaft in order to deface it. The light from below was still filling the rock tube, but the father she got from it, the harder it was to see. The graffiti started to fade into a gray dullness about three-quarters of the way up. The light below her was ever so faint. The fire was almost out, but then, so was she. She was grateful for the light she had. She wondered randomly, as the last of the light below her flickered and died, if burning scriptures was a sin. Then she decided that this particular set had truly provided light in the midst of darkness. Maybe it was their sole purpose while on this earth.

Using just the strength of her arms and a fortitude that surprised her, she ascended the last few feet of the mine shaft. Turning around, she found herself sitting on the top, her legs hanging back into the darkness. She pulled the matches out of her pocket and lit one. The match burst into flame, and she held it up while she counted the remaining matches in the small box. There were nineteen. She felt the fire creep toward her fingers and shook it before she burned herself.

She would have to hurry, but not so fast that the matches would blow out while she scurried toward the entrance. She stood up and lit a match. Quickly, she walked in the flickering light toward the mouth of the cave. She could walk approximately twenty paces before the match went out. As she turned, she knew she was getting closer to the entrance because she could feel a slight breeze. She was surprised that the breeze didn't affect the matches one way or the other. Then she remembered they were the waterproof girls' camp kind—leftovers from when she'd helped out at a fourth-year girls' camp clinic.

She only used ten matches to get to the cave entrance. Blessed moonlight shown down on the scrubby landscape of the Utah desert. In many places, the Salt Lake Valley really had blossomed like a rose but not on this lonely hillside outside of Hunter. She stopped for only the briefest of moments while she listened to the night. She could hear sirens in the distance—an excellent sign. The good guys were coming.

She hurried down the hill toward the gravel road as fast as her brother's shoes could take her. When she got to the side road, she could see the blue and white flashes of emergency vehicles over the top of the rolling hills. She prayed they were police cars and not ambulances. She tried to run and tripped. Ben's size twelve shoes and gravity got in her way. Her knees hit first, and she reached out her arms to break the fall, but her chin bounced on a boulder anyway. She pushed herself off the ground and wiped her chin with the back of her hand. The blood was ample and probably red, but in the moonlight, it took on the appearance of thin chocolate. She reached down and brushed the little pebbles off her knee.

Up again, she tried to trot as fast as she was able. She didn't yell out, because she wasn't sure of the who, what, when, and where of the situation.

Every few seconds, she swiped her chin. She was surprised at how much blood there was. She could feel it drizzling down her neck toward Ben's sweatshirt.

There was a slight rise in the road; she slowed as she ascended it. Once on top she could see the flashing lights. Headlights of police cars illuminated Ben's truck. They had opened the truck door and appeared to be crawling inside it.

"Hey!" she screamed. "Over here!"

Someone turned a bright light her way, and she squinted and immediately shielded her eyes.

"My name is Enin Woodson and this crazy guy kidnapped me because he was looking for Lance's gun but then Lance found me and we ran away but then he fell in a hole in the cave and you have to come help him and you have to come right now because he's hurt and he saved my life and now you've got to save his." Enin yelled down toward the crowd without so much as a breath of air between thoughts.

Two policemen came running toward her.

She recognized Bishop Butler right away. He stood out of the crowd because of his black suit, white shirt, and tie. She ran toward him. She didn't know the other guy.

She fell into her bishop's arms and began to speak between sobs. "Oh, Bishop, we have to go help Lance. I left him in the cave and . . ." she sucked in a breath of air, "he has a broken leg and his face is smashed against a rock, so he can't even speak."

She stopped to catch her breath and then slowly pushed herself away from Bishop Butler, blood staining the front of his white shirt. She looked to the left and then slowly to the right.

"Where's Ben?" she said.

Deputy Butler looked at A.J. and then back at Enin.

"What? Where's Ben?" She looked from her bishop to the other officer, her voice rising in pitch.

"You're brother's fine. He was shot in the arm and is on his way to the hospital right now. He's the one who led us here."

"Shot?" She looked at A.J. "Shot by who? That creep who kidnapped me? Where is he?" She looked at the cars around her. "You got him, right? You got the guy who kidnapped me, right?"

"Not yet, Enin. He's not here. He must have taken off after the confrontation with Ben," Deputy Butler said.

"What about Blake? Is Blake okay? The guy was going back to get the gun. Lance said he probably thinks Blake has it."

"Blake is fine. He's staying with your parents. Jared too."

"Okay. And Ben is going to be okay?"

"Yes, he lost some blood, but the wound wasn't very deep. He's on his way to Pioneer Hospital. You're parents will meet the ambulance there."

"Oh gosh, my parents! My mom must be going crazy. Maybe I should call her, but first you have to come with me to the cave. Lance is really, really hurt." She tugged on Deputy Butler's arm and tried to pull him back toward the cave.

"Enin, slow down, honey. If we need to do a rescue in a cave, we are going to need more than we have here. We have to call out fire and rescue."

"But I don't know if he has that much time. Can't you at

least try to help now?" Her voice cracked and she choked back a sob.

"Of course we will," A.J. said. He motioned to two men out of the crowd that had gathered to come over. "I want you," he said, pointing to the taller of the two men, "to follow Deputy Butler and me to the cave and then call in our exact location." Turning to an officer, he said, "You're in charge here. Protect the scene, and keep in radio contact. Oh, and call the Woodsons, and let them know we have Enin."

Both deputies nodded and motioned for the others to follow.

"Instead of walking, let's take the four-wheel drive vehicle. I take it the cave is off the beaten path."

Enin nodded, her lower lip in her mouth. Her chin had stopped dripping blood, but it was still shiny wet.

Chapter

27

"I think I hit a deer," Wayne Roy said in short quiet puffs to the older gentleman in the rumpled overalls, sports coat, white shirt, and tie, standing in front of him.

"Are you hurt?" the man asked, his head tilting to one side, inspecting the bloodied, disheveled man wobbling before his car's headlights. Only moments before had found the old farmer screeching to a stop ten feet in front of Wayne, fishtailing rubber from his truck on the top of the normally deserted highway.

Wayne Roy just looked at the man, his eyes trying to focus but failing. Tilting his own head to match the older man's, he put both hands on his temples. "Yeah, my head hurts."

The gentleman in the tie looked north up the road and then south from where he had just come. There was no traffic in either direction, which was normal for 4 A.M. on a Monday morning. Pulling off his sports coat, he put it around Wayne's shoulders and said, "Well, I think we better get you some help, buddy."

Wayne didn't fight the man. He let himself be gently led to the late seventies Chevy truck parked awkwardly in the center of the road. The man had to slam the passenger door twice to get it to latch.

Wayne looked briefly around the interior of the cab. It was clean on the inside. No Coke cans or candy wrappers littered the floors. A tiny little pine-scented tree hung from the rearview mirror.

The man in the tie got in and readjusted his mirror out of habit.

"Marge said, 'Get a cell phone, Floyd,' but do I listen? No, and now looky here, you're all cut and bloodied up, and there's no way to call an ambulance. I'm just gonna have to take you to the ER myself," the man said and shook his head in frustration.

Wayne turned his head slowly to look at the man. He didn't answer but put his head on the neoprene covered headrest and sighed.

"That's good, buddy, you just lie there. We'll get you some help."

Wayne heard muffled words, but they sounded like they were coming from a great distance away. He shut his eyes, only to snap them open at the searing pain in the right side of his head. His hands flew to his head, and he moaned.

The man in the tie pulled his car around and headed south toward the hospital. "Stay with me, buddy. I'll get you there as fast as this old truck can go."

Wayne rocked to and fro, his head rhythmically tapping on the dashboard.

Chapter 28

Lance was passing time by doing a body check. Stripped of all visual and auditory clues, he had to internally feel and assess each body system. Lance kept his eyes closed, grateful he could. He could blink, and the occasional tears helped wash away the grit and dust from the contacts he couldn't remove. His face was being pushed into the face of a rock, his mouth held in place by another rock behind his head. His body had lodged itself in a funnel shaped hole, his torso from below his arms hanging limply in space. He was fairly certain that one of his legs was broken, based on the searing, throbbing pain—but then again, he was grateful for the pain because he knew he was alive.

His right arm was wedged along what appeared to be a shelf, with debris from the fall stacked on it. The rubble was not heavy exactly, but right above the rock fragment was a flat stone that bridged the space. Even if he could remove the small rock and stone, he still was impacted by the larger rock above it. However, he could wiggle his fingers and move his arm slightly to and fro, so he counted that as a plus. How he managed to hold on to the flashlight was beyond him, but there it was in the one hand that actually had mobility. He could turn it on and off and move it to and fro.

His other arm was pinned awkwardly at an angle on the other side of the shelf. It was covered in heavier rubble and was beginning to ache from lack of movement.

He felt the most pressure on his back and rib cage. The weight of his body kept him wedged in the funnel. As long as the shelf didn't give way, he might make it until Enin returned with help—but realistically, where was she going to find it?

He had been praying on and off since Enin first asked him. He found he wasn't as frightened for himself as he was for Enin, and it was easier to ask for help for Enin than for himself. Not that he didn't ask for help to get out, but it wasn't like he was trying to make up for his past behaviors by begging for help now—that whole deathbed repentance thing.

Well, he supposed he was as close to a deathbed repentance as most people ever got, but he didn't want to come to the Lord from that position. He couldn't make the Lord come to his rescue when this whole thing was his fault anyway—but help for Enin—now that was a different story.

As he hung silently, he wondered if maybe this *was* going to be the worst day of his life, though that seemed next to impossible.

He was six, yet he remembered well the day his stepdad came and got him out of Mrs. Palmer's first grade class. He saw his stepdad walking past the windows toward the office during reading. A few minutes later, the principal came in and motioned for his teacher to come outside.

"Boys and girls, I need to speak with Principal Brown for a moment. I'll be right outside the window. Please keep your books open and read on your own for a minute." With that, she exited the room and stood talking to the principal.

At one point, her hand had flown to her mouth and stayed there for the rest of the conversation. When she walked back in the room, she was pale and visibly shook up.

"Class, Principal Brown is going to be helping you with the rest of your reading assignment."

His classmates, at five and six, were too young to have much of an opinion on that, so they just sat quietly and didn't ask questions. Then Mrs. Palmer walked over to him and bent down beside his miniature desk.

"Lance, we need to go to the office. Your dad is here to take you home," Mrs. Palmer said quietly.

Lance had just looked at her, his head tilted to one side. She looked like she was crying. *Why would his teacher be crying?*

"Honey, why don't you put your books and things away. Your dad is waiting."

"What about lunch?" Lance had asked practically.

"Lunch? Well, I think your dad will get you that. Come on now," and she gently started to put his books and pencils in the cubby under his desktop.

"Why is my dad here?" Lance asked suspiciously.

"He'll tell you in the office, honey." Mrs. Palmer stood and took his small hand in hers. He remembered how gently she held it.

"Am I in trouble?"

"Oh, no, honey. You haven't done anything wrong."

"Then why is my dad here?"

"He just needs to take you home."

"Why?"

"Let's go to the office and find out, okay," and she gently led him from the room, glancing up at Principal Brown and smiling weakly.

Down the corridor of the open hallway, she held his hand. Her hands were getting sweaty.

In the office, he could see his dad sitting in the principal's room. His back was to Lance, and he was bent over. Lance was having a hard time understanding why his dad was even here.

His mom always picked him up if he had a doctor's appointment or something like that. Why was his dad here?

"Dad? Where's Mommy?"

At this, his dad turned, and Lance was startled to see his dad's face puffed up with splotches of red. Was his dad crying? Dads don't cry. His dad never cried. He got mad and yelled sometimes, but moms cry, not dads.

His dad motioned for him to come closer. Lance did. His dad lifted him up on his lap, wrapped his arms around him too tightly, and started to sob. He started to rock Lance back and forth on his lap. Lance sat motionless, he turned once to his teacher, but she was now openly crying. The school secretary was in the doorway crying as well.

"What's the matter?" Lance asked of the adults around him. He was getting frightened.

"Dad? Where's Mommy?" he asked again.

His dad stopped rocking and straightened up. He put both hands on Lance's shoulders and said softly, "Lance. Your mother was in a car accident this morning, and she . . . well, honey, she died."

Lance just stared at his dad. He didn't say a thing. The room was uncomfortably silent.

Mrs. Palmer bent down next to him. "Do you know what that means, honey?"

Lance shrugged his shoulders and then nodded his head that he did. That was the beginning of the worst day of his life—including today.

Lance could feel the hot tears running down his cheeks, and then he could taste them. Drizzling toward his open mouth, they were filled with salt and the grit of the cave. His mind wandered back to his father—his Father in Heaven, that is. His whole life he had heard that people who found themselves in these extreme experiences usually learned some great lesson from it. He even could remember that Joseph Smith had been told in Liberty Jail that these kinds of things would give him experience.

He thought back to early morning seminary when Brother Bates had really emphasized Doctrine and Covenants 122:7-8. In fact, there had been this challenge that anyone memorizing these two verses would receive a ten dollar coupon for In and Out Burgers. It was one of the more effective, but probably more expensive challenges Brother Bates had offered. Over one half of the class, himself included had memorized the two verses. Lance found he could recall the scriptures even now.

"And if thou should be cast into the pit," *check,* Lance thought, "or into the hands of murderers," *check again,* "and the sentence of death passed upon thee, if thou be cast into the deep;" *double check,* "if the billowing surge conspire against thee; if fierce winds become thine enemy; if the heavens gather blackness," *now this is getting too close* "and all the elements combine to hedge up the way; and above all, if the very jaws of hell shall gape open the mouth wide after thee . . ." *Oh my gosh. I'm actually in the very jaws of hell,* Lance thought as his eyes of understanding were beginning to clear. "Know thou, my son, that all these things shall give thee experience, and shall be for thy good. The Son of Man hath descended below them all. Art thou greater than he?"

Lance moved his shoulders with a start, instinctively reacting to his sudden understanding of the two scriptures that he was able to recall in their entirety. The abrupt movement of his shoulders caused the boulder behind his head to move slightly. It slipped toward the right and then gently landed on the other rock that was a bridge over his free arm, unpinning part of his head for the first time since he had plunged into his own form of outer darkness.

"Heavenly Father, please forgive me," were the first words out of his mouth when he could finally move his lips. His head was still pushed against the rock, but he could at least move his lips and whisper. He licked the salt and dirt from around his mouth. "I think I'm finally beginning to get it. Perhaps you would consider letting me live long enough to do something with this information." When he opened his eyes, he was astonished to see a dim light coming from the shaft leading toward freedom. The first words he heard were a soft, "Hang on, son."

Chapter

29

A.J. pulled a fast right off the gravel road at Enin's signal. Bouncing, the utility 4x4 dipped and shimmied along a dry creek bed toward a hill in the distance. The headlights alternately cast wild shadows upon the ground and onto the rapidly approaching boulders in the rising terrain. A.J. made an evasive maneuver as the headlights illuminated a rusted out station wagon leaning drunkenly on its side.

"We're almost there," Enin said as they passed the dilapidated station wagon. Pointing toward a metal grating, she began punching her finger in the air in front of her. "There. There. The cave's right there! Behind that metal gate."

A.J. put the truck into four-wheel drive and continued up the moderately steep incline. He parked on a flat area in front of the cave; the headlights illuminating a full twenty feet into the cave. With the parking brake secure, he unlatched his seat belt and reached under his seat to grab his twenty-four-inch combination nightstick and flashlight.

Enin followed Deputy Butler out.

"He's in here," she said, pulling on her bishop's arm, as she ran toward the opening.

"Easy, Enin, we need some light. Wait up for Sheriff Lanz."

A.J. followed closely behind them.

"How far in?" A.J. asked Enin.

"Not too far. Can I use your flashlight?" she said, reaching out to take it from the sheriff.

A.J. handed it to her and she walked as quickly as she could toward the back reaches of the cavern. When they got to the mine shaft, she stopped and pointed the light down it.

She handed the light to the sheriff and turned to enter the shaft backward as she had done earlier that evening.

"Ah, no, I don't think that's such a good idea," A.J. said, looking at the size twelve shoes she was still wearing. "Why don't I go down and assess the situation? You and Deputy Butler stay up here and wait for the rescue squad. You did say the floor had caved in, right?"

"Well, right . . . but . . ." Enin began.

"So maybe it's not such a good idea for a lot of people to go down there. If he's as stuck as you say, he's going to need someone stronger to help him out, right?"

"Yeah, I guess . . . but . . ."

"So let me go down. You and Butler stay here. I doubt if I'm going to get good reception down in the cavern anyway. I'll need you here so I can relay messages to the rescue unit." A.J. was trying but not really succeeding in making Enin feel like this was a team effort. The reality was: the last thing A.J. wanted was an emotionally overwrought girlfriend getting in the way of a dangerous rescue operation. Besides, he still wasn't clear on what this kid's real motives were before he got trapped. There was a lot to sort out, and he didn't need or want Enin coming.

He jammed the light in a place on his belt and started to step on the first rung of the steeply angled planks, putting his hands on either side of the wall.

"It's easier if you turn around and go down backward. Oh, and if you keep your feet toward the outside edges. Also, there's a broken board about halfway down," Enin said helpfully.

A.J. did as suggested.

It was a long way down. As he got about halfway, he could hear the strained voice of someone below. He knew when he got to the broken plank because his feet caught it at a funny angle. He took the next few planks very carefully.

He leaned slightly over his shoulder and directed his voice downward, "Hang on, son."

A.J. finished his descent and felt his feet on solid ground. Well, he wasn't sure how solid the ground really was when his flashlight caught sight of the fifteen-foot-wide gaping hole in the middle of the cave floor. He got himself into a prone position on the rock-covered floor and crawled toward the open scar in the earth. The boy in the pit kept the light steady; its dim beam showed his location some four feet below A.J.'s shoulders.

"I'm Sheriff Lanz, and I'll be helping you out of here," A.J. said.

"Actually, hanging on is all I'm able to do at this point anyway," the boy said in a slightly muffled voice.

"Right. Maybe not the best choice of words," A.J. said as he turned his long, brighter than average flashlight toward the young man's position.

"Ouch," said A.J. when he saw the youth for the first time. He was pinned under what looked to be a half a yard of rock and rubble that reminded him of a mutated Jenga puzzle. There were many places to start pulling the rubble off, but any one rock looked like it could potentially bring the rest of the rock crashing down on his head and partially covered arms. It was going to be a slow rescue at best.

"Ditto," was the young man's soft reply.

"Can you give me an idea where you might be hurt?"

"My right leg. It's hanging below me in the other cave. I

can feel it and move it at the knee but it hurts pretty bad. It's like throbbing and stuff," the boy said.

"What do you mean 'other cave'?" A.J. asked.

"When I fell, I broke through to the sort of cave you see me in, but the fall must have pierced through the roof of another cavern below that. I'm more or less lodged in the opening of the top of the next cave down."

"Okay," A.J. said slowly, trying to figure out what to do next. "So you're a cork?"

"Maybe more like stuff jamming a funnel," the boy countered.

"How much of you is dangling then?"

"From my chest down. My arms and shoulders are keeping me here and while I'm not hurt too badly—except for my leg—my arms and shoulders are beginning to cramp."

"I'll bet." A.J. moved the bright beam around the loose rock that was pinning the boy. He couldn't see the young man's face because of the way the youth was lodged in the hole. He had to listen closely when the boy spoke because he was talking into the face of a small boulder. Inspecting the area around his partially exposed arm and head, it appeared the rock was not as deep as A.J. had originally thought.

"How's Enin?" the boy asked.

"She's okay. She's too worried about you to think about what she's just been through. She's probably also a little in shock, but she insisted on coming here first, and I can see why. How long have you two been together?"

"Enin and me?" the boy questioned A.J. He could hear the surprise in the young man's voice. "I just met her a couple of days ago."

"Oh, right. Sorry, I thought . . ."

The boy cut him off, "No problem. She's actually an amazing girl. I should be so lucky."

"Well, I think what we need to do here is get the top layer of rock off of you then get some rope under your arms and secure you while we pull away the rest of the rubble."

"That's what I came up with too," the boy replied.

"Okay, well then I'm going to go back up the tunnel about halfway so I can use my radio, but I'll still be close enough that you can yell if you need me."

"Hey, can you tell Enin I can talk now. When she left, my face was still plastered against one of these rocks. Tell her I'm pretty much okay and not to worry."

"Of course. I think because of the instability of these rocks I'm going to try to pull you out myself or maybe just get one more guy, but I don't want a bunch of people down here stomping around."

"I agree—especially about the stomping around part."

"Okay then, I'll be right back." A.J. slowly shimmied backward on his belly until he felt safe enough to stand, although *safe* was a relative word here. He was pretty sure the reason the cave had been gated and locked in the first place was because the owners feared this very kind of problem.

When A.J. was about halfway up the shaft, his two-way radio crackled to life.

"Butler? You copy?" A.J. said.

"Ten-four, A.J."

"Where are you?" A.J. asked.

"At the cave entrance. I brought Enin back out here to the unit. She was getting agitated not knowing what was happening with her friend. She's on the phone to her folks right now."

"Good call. What's the ETA on the rescue squad?"

"Fifteen minutes out."

"Good. Here's what I'm going to need . . ." A.J. briefed the deputy and then crawled back toward the captive in the cave.

After repositioning himself over the edge of the hole, he highlighted the boy's head. "Good news. The rescue rig is on its way, and they'll be sending their smallest guy down with the gear."

"What about water? I'm so stinking thirsty."

"Water too."

"Great," the boy said.

"Listen," A.J. said to the top of the boy's head, "while we're going to need to talk in depth about what's been going on in the past twenty-four hours, I'd rather wait until we get you out of here. So how 'bout we just pass the time with something more conversational?"

"Yeah okay, but I'm not much of a conversationalist."

A.J. started. "So I hear you're from California. You live there long?"

"My whole life. I was born near San Diego but only lived down there when I was really little. Most of my life has been spent in northern California."

"I lived near San Diego for a while too."

"Really. Where?"

"I was in boot camp at the MCRD in San Diego and then a few weeks at Camp Pendleton, near Oceanside."

"Camp Pendleton?"

"Yeah," A.J. said. "After boot camp. Beautiful place—really nice after what I'd just been through—boot camp was pretty rigorous."

"My mom worked there before I was born."

"On Pendleton? When?" A.J. asked, mildly surprised he had some connection with this man-child.

"Well, I was born in '85, so she must have worked there in '83 or '84. I don't know the exact dates or anything."

"Small world. I was there in '84 too. What did she do on base?"

"Worked in the com-com, uh, com-missionary or something like that."

"Do you mean the commissary?"

"Yeah, I guess. That's a grocery store or something like that, right?"

A.J. felt his stomach tighten involuntarily. "Uh . . . right . . . well it's more like a Super Wal-Mart for military families."

"She was a checker, I think."

At this piece of information, A.J. found himself gripping

the flashlight tighter. He could feel clammy perspiration against the cool metal. He took in a long, deep breath between clenched teeth. He was probably going to know this kid's mother, and this kid's mother was going to know her. He felt it in his bones.

A.J. closed his eyes and asked, "What's your mom's name?" hoping the kid below him couldn't hear the rising anxiety in his voice. He was struggling to maintain control of this unexpected situation.

"Belinda Morris."

A.J. bit his lower lip. His throat constricted and he could feel the rapidly increasing beat of his heart in his ears. Of all the possible names this kid could have given, this was the last one he expected. He was vaguely aware that the boy below him was speaking again. "Huh? I'm sorry, what'd you say?"

"I said, 'Do you think you might have ever seen her at the market?' I mean, did you shop there much?"

A.J. opened his mouth, then closed it, then opened his mouth, then closed it. On the third try, he heard himself say, "Yes, as a matter of fact, I knew her."

"Really? You knew my mom? Wow, that's weird isn't it?"

A.J. nodded his head in agreement, though the boy couldn't see the motion.

"Hey, I know this might sound weird, but would you mind telling me what you remember about her? I never really met anyone but my stepdad who knew her. That sounds weird, I know, but she was an only child and all."

A.J. was in the middle of rubbing the perspiration off his brow with his free arm but stopped, mid-rub. "I'm not sure I understand what you want. Run that by me again."

"Oh, I'm sorry. I probably left out a couple of important pieces. My mom died when I was six, and then my stepdad died a few years later. So I never really knew anyone who actually knew my mom. Anything you might remember about her would be okay. I'm not looking for a novel or anything; I know it was a long time ago."

A.J. didn't, or couldn't, reply. He felt a tear trickle down his cheek. *Dead? She was dead?*

"Sheriff, are you okay?" the boy asked.

A.J. could hear the concern in the voice below him.

"Yeah, I'm okay. I was just startled to hear your mom was gone. I'm sorry."

"How well did you know her?" the boy asked very slowly.

Clearly the boy could tell that A.J. was upset.

A.J. wasn't sure what to say. He finally offered, "Well, your mom and I actually dated."

"You dated my mom?" The boy's voice rose in pitch.

"Yeah. But only for a couple of weeks. Like I said, I had finished boot camp and there was a problem with me getting in the M.P. school. An instructor had a heart attack or something. I ended up being at Pendleton a few weeks longer than normal. We only went to the movies a few times. I think we saw *Ghostbusters* two, or maybe even three, times."

"So you would remember stuff about her, right?"

"Sure. I remember your mom," A.J. said quietly. "She was really funny. She had a great sense of humor, but she also had a stubborn streak. If she didn't want to go someplace, or do something, there was nothing you could do to change her mind."

A.J. heard a muffled laugh. "Yeah, that's what my stepdad used to say too, at least the part about Mom being stubborn."

"How'd she die?"

"Car accident."

"And your stepdad?"

"Cancer," the boy replied simply.

"I'm really sorry to hear that. Anyway, I met your mom through a friend. She was dating one of the cooks on base who sort of befriended me. Well, to be more exact, she was in this group of people my buddy used to hang out with. A bunch of us used to go out. My buddy ended up getting transferred to

☆

Biloxi, and I sort of kept hanging with the group. Then your mom and I went out a few times alone."

"Then what?"

"Well, then I headed for my military police training in Missouri, and your mom stayed in Oceanside."

"You didn't stay in contact with her?"

"Oh, we talked on the phone once or twice, but I only ever got one letter from her . . ." A.J.'s voice trailed off.

"Yeah, that sounds about right. I only have one letter from her too. I guess she wasn't much of a writer."

"I guess." A.J. thought back to the day he got the letter. His head was beginning to hurt, his throat was dry, and he needed air. "I, uh . . ." A.J. paused; he'd forgotten the kid's name. "I'm going to go up and see if that truck is here yet, okay, son? Actually, I'm sorry, but with all that's been going on, I've forgotten your name."

"My full name?" Lance asked.

"Right," A.J. said with a tight voice.

"No problem. My full name, if you add all my stepfathers is Lance Alma Morris-Andrews-Raintree." Lance said in almost a singsong tone.

The tone was lost on Sheriff *Alma Jacob Lanz*—A.J. for short. All he heard the boy say was "Lance Alma," and he could hear a young Belinda Morris whisper-cry in the phone, "I'm not going to keep this baby, A.J., I just can't." He'd believed her.

Chapter

30

"When can I talk to Ben?" Enin said into Bishop Butler's cell phone.

"He's in surgery right now, honey," her father replied.

"But I thought they said he was okay. I thought they said the bullet only grazed him. Why is he in surgery?"

"They have to make sure there's no muscle damage and close the wound."

"Did you talk to him before he went in? How is he? What did he say?"

"He was mostly concerned about you. He still doesn't know they found you and his friend. He kept asking us to pray for you two, which of course, no one had to ask *us* to do. We haven't stopped praying since this whole thing began."

"I'm so sorry, Daddy. I never meant to put you and Mom through this." Enin could feel hot tears running down her throat, and she dropped her head to her chest.

"Enin, don't you think for one minute that we blame you! Oh, and you'll appreciate this—he *asked* for a blessing before he went into surgery."

"Really?" Enin lifted her head. "A blessing? That's wonderful. A blessing . . ." Her voice trailed off and then picked up. "Did he say what happened, or who shot him?"

"He didn't know who shot him. It was pretty dark."

"I'll bet it was the creep from the house."

"That's the sheriff's guess too. Someone told me they found your shoes in the campground."

"My shoes! I forgot all about them. I've been wearing Ben's."

"Ben's shoes?"

"Yeah, sounds weird I know, but you don't know how grateful I am for his smelly old Sketchers."

"How's Ben's friend? I heard he was hurt pretty bad."

"Lance? They're with him right now. They're trying to get him out. They won't let me help, but I keep telling them I'm the smallest one around, and I could go down the hole."

"Well, honey, I'm going to have to agree with them. You may be the smallest there, but you've just been through some pretty tough stuff yourself. Just let the fire department handle it."

"I'm trying, but I'm really scared for Lance. He saved my life, Daddy. Did I tell you that? I mean, he literally saved my life."

"That's what I hear. I also heard you won't let them take you to get checked out."

"I'm not leaving here without Lance. I can't. He never left my side. He stayed with me the whole time. I'm not leaving until they bring him out of there."

"But, honey . . ."

"No, Daddy. I won't go without him. I promised him. I'm okay, really. I know you think that I'm not thinking clearly because I've just been through a kidnapping and all, but I promise you, I'm okay for now. Maybe later I'll break down, but for now I'm more concerned about Lance. The creep who took me didn't do anything physical to me. He was kind of a sad wacko. He locked me in a stinky outhouse all day, but as scared as I was, I always knew I would get out of there. I'll admit I didn't think I'd be rescued by Lance, but looking back, it makes perfect sense."

"Well, how long until they get your friend out?"

"Bishop told me they were close to pulling him up. They had a lot of rock to move, and I guess they're having to go pretty slowly because the ground may not be stable. There are a lot of firemen here now. Hey, wait . . ." Enin turned toward some commotion in the front of the cave. She could see lights filling the cave entrance and saw two firemen on either side of a stretcher exiting. "I've got to go, Daddy. I'll call you later. They just brought Lance out."

"Okay, honey. Call me back as soon as you can."

"Okay," she said, snapping the phone shut. Running toward the stretcher, she pocketed the bishop's phone in her pants.

"Lance," she said breathlessly, "are you okay?" She looked down onto a face covered in crusted bits of dried blood and dirt and grimaced. "Oh, you don't look so good."

"Thanks," Lance said.

"Well, actually you look great. You look wonderful. I've been so worried about you. I was so mad they wouldn't let me go down there. I've . . ."

"Slow down, Enin," Lance said and sort of reached out one free hand to her. His whole body was being immobilized by two-inch-wide straps crisscrossing his torso and legs. His head and neck were in a cushioned neck brace, but he could get one hand loose and reach out.

She took it and held his hand in both of hers. Walking alongside of the bright yellow backboard they had him strapped to was awkward but not impossible.

"Where are you taking him?" she asked the firemen.

"Pioneer Hospital."

☆

"Can I ride in the ambulance?"

"Actually," Enin heard Bishop Butler's voice behind her, "we were kind of hoping you would. We need to get you seen by a doctor too."

"I'm okay to go now that you have Lance out, but I want to go with him."

Deputy Butler caught the eye of one of the paramedics and nodded his approval. The paramedic nodded back.

"Okay. We'll follow behind you," Deputy Butler said.

A pale orange, ice cream-colored sky was beginning to reveal itself in the east. Enin walked carefully down the slope from the cave entrance to a waiting ambulance, never releasing Lance's hand. For the sake of balance, she had dropped one of her hands, but the other one was now interlaced with Lance's.

The paramedics made her release his hand while they transferred Lance onto a padded stretcher in the ambulance. After they had him restrapped, they invited her to step inside and sit at Lance's side.

"So that was crazy, wasn't it?" Enin said. She had to bend over slightly to look at Lance in the eyes. His hand was in her's again. His head was facing straight up, and he couldn't look at her.

"Yeah, crazy," he agreed and then continued. "So what was all the shooting about? Did you hear?"

"They think it was the crazy guy. He shot Ben in the arm."

"Ben! What was Ben doing here?" Lance said.

"I guess looking for us."

"How would he know where to find us?"

"I guess the same way you knew."

Lance was silent for a moment; then he slowly said, "Oh, right."

"That whole Spirit thing," Enin voiced unnecessarily.

"Yeah, that whole Spirit thing. I've noticed that whole Spirit thing follows you around, Enin."

☆

"Me? Not just me, Lance. All of us. You and Ben and Blake and Jared. If you think about what could have happened, and then all that *only* happened, I think we've been pretty blessed."

"You're so funny, Enin. Only you could think that getting kidnapped, getting shot, and falling through a cave was a blessing."

"Lance, I'm not dead, you're not dead, Ben's not dead, and Blake and Jared escaped the creep completely. Given what could have happened, yeah, I think we're pretty blessed."

"Alright, I concede your point."

"Are you saying you don't think we've been protected?"

"No. I'm agreeing with you, really," and he was.

"Oh, guess what? Ben asked my dad for a blessing."

"Doesn't surprise me."

"It did me," Enin said.

"It shouldn't. Ben is a lot more spiritual than you give him credit. I saw him that day at Mandy's, remember?"

"Wasn't that just yesterday?" Enin asked, puzzled.

"Oh yeah, it was. Wow, it seems like it was days ago."

The ambulance lurched forward, and Enin almost hit her head on the top of Lance's.

"Sorry," she said.

"No problem. I thought you were bending down to kiss me." Lance smiled a crooked little smile.

"You wish," Enin said.

"Maybe."

Enin blushed.

"We certainly have been through a lot these past couple of days, haven't we?" Enin said thoughtfully.

"Uh, duh?" Lance replied sarcastically.

"No, I mean it."

"I do too. We have been, and I have a feeling it's not over. At least I hope it's not over."

"What?" Enin asked. Understanding then filled her eyes, and she blushed.

Lance turned his eyes away from Enin, suddenly embarrassed that he might have said too much.

Enin squeezed Lance's hand slightly in response, and then she looked at him a moment before she bent over and dusted his lips ever so lightly with hers.

He closed his eyes and smiled a crooked little smile. Then he said, "That was nice."

"I'm glad. It was my first one."

Lance's eyes quickly opened in wonder. "Say again."

Enin shook her head, embarrassed.

"You've never kissed anyone?"

Enin shook her head in the negative.

"And how old are you?"

"You know I'm twenty."

"And you've never kissed or been kissed?"

"So stop rubbing it in already. No, I've never been kissed. Hey, I'm a good girl, remember?"

"I'm just surprised."

"Why? I told you I didn't really appeal to most boys, and since boys are who'd I'd kiss, I've never had one kiss me."

"But you've dated, right?"

"Not really, at least not like some guy called me on the phone and asked me to go somewhere—like the movies or bowling."

"What about school dances?" Lance said, still trying to wrap his mind around the emerging fact that Enin hadn't dated.

"I went with Ben to my prom, but only because I didn't want to go alone. I could have gone alone; some of my friends did. I took Ben and me and my friends shared him."

"But you're so cute," Lance said in wonder.

"Must be my annoying personality then," Enin said sharply.

"I didn't mean it that way."

Enin shrugged. "I know. I'm not mad, just a little sad. I would like to have dated more, but the opportunity never came up."

"It will, trust me."

Enin blushed again.

"That is, if I can just get over your annoying personality," Lance said, smiling broadly despite his bruised and scraped-up face.

Chapter

31

"Sorry to wake you up, but I had to talk to you," A.J. said to his wife.

"It's okay, A.J. What's up?" she said sleepily.

"I don't know quite how to tell you this . . ." he started.

"What?" Her voice was at full attention now.

"Melanie, you aren't going to believe this; I hardly believe it myself," A.J. said, his voice tight with emotion.

"A.J., what is it?" He could hear the panic rising in his wife's voice.

"She didn't have the abortion."

"Who didn't have an abortion?"

"Belinda. Belinda Morris. The girl in California. She didn't have the abortion."

"A.J., what are you talking about? How do you know she didn't have it? You said she sent you a letter. You said . . ."

A.J. cut her off. "I know what I said, but I was wrong. She

had the baby. She never told me."

"Did you have another dream? How do you know this?"

"Because I met him tonight, in the cave. He was in the cave. He was the boy I had to rescue. It was my son."

"What cave? The last I heard you were at a girl's house, and they thought she'd been kidnapped."

"I was, and then her brother called to say they found his truck. Then the brother got shot. When we went to investigate, the girl who'd been kidnapped showed up and said there was this kid who'd fallen in a hole in a cave. I went in to assess the situation, and I discovered he was my son."

"A.J., that's crazy. You can't know that."

"I do. I know it. I was talking to him to keep him calm. We started talking about mundane stuff, like where he was born, and it turned out he was born in San Diego in 1985."

"Lots of people were born in San Diego that year. That doesn't make him your long lost son."

"I'm not done. He was born in 1985 to Belinda Morris— my old girlfriend. Belinda Morris had the baby, and she named him *Lance*. Lance Alma Morris."

There was no response on the other end of the line.

"Mel? You still there?" A.J. asked.

"Yes," a quiet voice responded. "Does he know? Did you tell him?"

"Gosh, no. The kid was stuck in a pile of rocks. I didn't even know if he was going to make it until a few minutes ago. He's on his way to Pioneer Hospital now."

"Well, what are you going to do?"

"I don't know. That's why I called you."

"Okay, let me call my mom to come over. I'll meet you at the hospital. We can figure it out there. I think you'll have to have DNA tests or something. How do you feel?"

"Scared."

"Me too. I guess we'll have to deal with his mother soon enough."

"Oh, no. I'm so flipped out right now, I didn't tell you that

Belinda died when he was six. Then his stepfather died a few years later. He's being raised by his stepmother and her new husband. He evidently was having problems at home and that's why he ended up in Utah."

"You're kidding."

"No. For all intents and purposes, he has no earthly family. Just call your mom and hurry. I can't do this alone."

"I will," she said.

"Thanks for being there for me."

"A.J.?"

"What?"

"All those dreams, all those years. They were really visions."

"I know. I haven't been able to stopping thinking about that very same thing," A.J. said, and he wiped at both of his eyes with the back of his dirty hand. "Melanie, he needed me then, but now he needs us both."

"I know" was the simple reply.

A.J. put the phone back in his pocket and stared at the emerging dawn over the hills. Rubbing his arms with his hands was in response to emotion rather that chill. It was only about fifty-five degrees out.

He turned back toward the cave entrance when he heard his named being called.

"Over here," he said to Deputy Butler.

"They found a rolled gray Taurus with California plates about two miles from here. Some kids called it in."

"Was the perp in it?"

"No, they haven't been able to locate him yet. There was no one in or around the car, except for the deer he hit."

"You're saying he walked away?" A.J. said.

"Maybe. Maybe he hitchhiked out. We don't know. All we know is he's not there."

"We have to put out an all-points bulletin. This guy is not stable. He's already kidnapped a girl and then shot someone else; he's a loose cannon."

"Agreed. The FBI is up on the main road. What do you

want us to do with them?"

"I'm heading out that way to the hospital. I'll talk to them when I pass. I want you to stay here long enough to get the grate locked back up on this entrance and then meet me at the hospital."

"Right. Do you mind if I go home and change into my uniform first?" Butler asked.

"That's fine. You can bill the department for cleaning the suit."

"Not necessary, but thanks anyway, it's part of my other job."

"That's right, you're these kids' bishop, aren't you?"

"Yes."

"All the more reason for you to get to the hospital ASAP. You have at least two members of your ward being admitted right now."

Bishop Butler nodded gravely. "I'm well aware of that. I'll see you in a bit."

Chapter

32

Ben opened one eye slowly. He couldn't manage to get the other one to cooperate. They were both so very heavy.

He could dimly see the peach yogurt-colored walls in the pale, early light of morning. At least he thought it was morning. He supposed it could be dusk. He was not totally aware of the time. He laboriously turned his head to the left. There was a large computer thingy next to him, humming and occasionally beeping. He coughed and the machine beeped in response.

He yawned and realized he had plastic tubing coming out of his nose. He wiggled his nose and noted that the tubing was taped to his face.

His head itched. He mentally told his arm to reach up and scratch it, but his arm could not cooperate, it too was restrained. The act of trying to lift it caused a searing pain to rush through his body.

Oh yeah, I've been shot. How weird is that?

A curtain was drawn part way around his bed. He could see a little part of a person whom he assumed must be a nurse.

"Hello?" he said in a small, unfamiliar voice.

The person turned toward him. It was his sister Sariah. He was surprised to see her. She was a nurse but in a convalescent hospital. She had on her dark purple pants and funky nurses top with little pastel stethoscopes on it that she frequently wore to family dinners on Sundays when she had to work.

"You're awake," she said, smiling at him.

"I guess. I'm not too awake though. I think they must have given me something. I feel really weird right now."

"Yeah, must be the Demerol. It'll wear off. You nauseated at all?"

He closed his eyes to feel his body. "No, I don't think so. I just feel . . ."

"Drugged?"

"I guess. I feel like I took a double dose of NyQuil."

"Yeah, that would be about right."

"How come you're here? Or," Ben looked more closely at the room, "am I at your place?" he said questioningly.

Sariah laughed. "Gosh no, we don't get too many gunshot patients at Happy Hills Convalescent. You're at Pioneer."

"Oh, well are Mom and Dad here?"

"Of course. They're down the hall. I was just going to go get them. We've been waiting for you to wake up."

"Yeah, would you? I need to talk to Mom."

"Sure." Sariah turned and left Ben with the quietly humming machine.

Ben's mother rushed in, followed by his father, and what seemed like a few thousand other siblings.

"Happy Birthday, Mom."

His mother reached down and kissed him on the cheek. "Thank you. I'm surprised you remembered with all that's gone on. They've had you pretty doped up these past few hours." She reached down and held his good hand.

He squeezed her hand lightly in return. "Yeah, I know, but it's all coming back. Any news about Enin or Lance?"

The crowd around his bed grinned collectively.

"What?" Ben asked, eyeing the entire group but settling on his dad.

"Enin's fine. In fact, she's down the hall now in Emergency. We just left her. She'll be here as soon as they get done talking with her. They asked us to step out. All these new privacy laws are getting a bit ridiculous," Mosiah said.

"What happened? Was she really kidnapped?"

"Yes, she really was, but evidently your new friend Lance found her, and they both escaped. They turned up a little bit after you got shot, but by then you were in surgery."

"So how's Lance?"

"So-so. They brought him and Enin in together. He may have broken his leg in a couple of places when he fell through the cave floor."

"What cave?"

"I'll let Enin tell you about it when she gets up here. She can't wait to see you. She's been worried sick. Well, we've all been worried sick, not just Enin."

"That's great. Hey, if you guys don't mind," he said, turning to his siblings, "I need to talk to Mom and Dad—sort of alone."

With some "sures," "no problems," and an "okay" or two, the crowd of relatives left Ben alone with his folks.

"What's up?" Mosiah asked, concern evident in his tightening voice.

"This has been a weird weekend," Ben began.

"Agreed," said his father.

"I saw Mandy's great-grandmother yesterday."

"Sister Parker?" His parents both looked at each other, their brows furrowing in unison.

"Yeah, Sister Parker. She's the blind lady who lived around the corner from Mandy."

"We know who she is. She used to be the stake Relief

Society president," his mother said.

Ben shrugged and then winced in pain. "Ouch. I have to stop doing that. Anyway, I didn't know that. I just know she's a sweet old lady, but yesterday, boy, did I get a dressing down from her."

"When did you speak to her?"

"About two. Why?" Ben asked, suddenly aware of his father's incessant nervous tapping on his bed.

"Sister Parker passed away last night," his mother said quietly.

"What? You're kidding. How? When?"

His mother continued. "It was before all this happened with your sister and you. Two deacons went over to pass the sacrament and they found her. They thought she was sleeping. When they shook her and she didn't wake up, they went out and got their adviser who called 911, but she was already gone."

Ben closed his eyes. This put a whole new spin on things, or did it? Wasn't what he was about to tell his parents still valid. Hadn't he indeed had a mighty change of heart? Perhaps he was led to Sister Parker's right then *because* she wasn't going to be here long.

"What were you doing over there?" Mosiah asked.

"I went to get my old letters and stuff from Mandy's. She said it was in her closet. When I got there, it turns out Sister Parker was staying in Mandy's old room. She thought Lance and I were the deacons coming to pass the sacrament. When she found out it was me, she really laid into me."

"For what?" his mother said, surprised that Sister Parker knew her son well enough to chastise him two years after he had broken up with Mandy.

"For letting my breakup with Mandy affect how I was now living my life, I guess. She didn't cut me any slack. She said I was 'prideful.' She was right. I've let the whole Mandy thing color my life for too long."

"So what are you saying, Ben?" Mosiah gently asked the question that was hanging on his wife's lips.

"I guess I'm saying I'm ready to talk to the bishop. I'm tired of fighting who I am. I'm not some punk kid off the street. I'm Ben, and while I'm far from who I want to be, or who you guys may want me to be, I'm tentatively ready to come back, and before you think that this is the drugs talking, it's not. This is me. I've been thinking about this for a long time. Before Lance showed up, before I talked to Sister Parker, before I got shot." Ben paused and then continued, "I think this is the part where you're suppose to cry, Mom."

"Right, but I think you actually shocked the tears right out of me this time," she said honestly.

"Happy Birthday, Mom." Ben smiled a bent little smile at his mom.

His mother squeezed his good hand slightly and then jumped at what sounded like the muffled backfire of a car.

Ben knew better.

Chapter

33

"Hey, A.J., haven't seen you in a while. What brings you down here?" Dr. Taylor asked, glancing up from the hospital documents he was working on.

"The gunshot you got in a little earlier tonight, and then the other two kids a few minutes ago—same case."

"Wow, someone's had a busy night. You catch the bad guys yet?"

"Nope. We have an APB out, but nothing so far. We think he may have hitchhiked back to California. We've notified Nevada and California—but what are they going to do? Until the perp does something stupid again they're pretty much in the dark too."

"Yeah, agreed. So who's this?" Dr. Taylor said, motioning to the petite, dark-haired woman at A.J.'s side.

"Oh, I'm sorry, this is my wife, Melanie."

"So is this is a personal visit as opposed to a work visit?" Dr. Taylor asked.

"It's a little hard to explain, but both, actually. So I'm really glad you're the one on this morning. I need to talk to you in private. Well, actually, we need to talk to you. We have a delicate problem, and I'm hoping you can help."

"Sure. I take it we need a little more privacy than this room affords?" the doctor said, looking at the eight or so medical personnel flitting around the main desk of the ER.

"Yeah" was A.J.'s one-word reply.

A.J. and Melanie followed Dr. Taylor into what might have been a closet before but was now a poor excuse for an office. It housed two computers and a copy machine.

"Medical records. They don't use this room for another hour or so. What's up?"

"I'm not sure how to even begin . . ." A.J. began for the second time this evening.

Fifteen minutes later, Dr. Taylor was leaning against the copy machine, rubbing the side of his stubbled face. "Wow," he said, and then he rubbed the other side of his face and said, "Wow," again.

"I know. That's why I came to you." A.J. looked at his friend hopefully.

"Wow," Dr. Taylor said for the third time.

"Stop with the 'wow' already, you're making me feel like a heel."

"Am I?" Dr. Taylor said quizzically. "Nothing could be further from my mind. I was just marveling at how everything came together. It's pretty cool if you think about it. Think of all that had to be set in place for you to meet your son, and at this point, I suspect you're right that he is your son. This isn't about a set of coincidences—this is the real deal. Hey, you could get a write-up on the back of the *Church News* with this story."

A.J. shook his head and rolled his eyes at his friend. Melanie had been quiet the entire time, but even she pulled her eyebrows together at the last suggestion he made.

"So how old is he again?" Dr. Taylor asked.

"Twenty-one."

"Well, legally you can speak to him without his parents, or stepparents, as the case may be. I suppose that just leaves the question of how and when."

"His stepmom is on her way. I think she said something about being here about ten, yet I don't get the feeling I should wait for her."

"Well, buddy, at this point I'd go with your gut feelings. You've been right so far, and I have a feeling that you're still being guided."

"Will you come in there with us?"

"Of course, but wouldn't you rather have a psychologist? We have one on call."

"No. I think I just need some moral support and a little medical backing. I was hoping you could explain the genetics thing."

"Sure, A.J." Dr. Taylor then looked at Melanie. "How are you with all of this?"

"Well, I've always known about Belinda, and we've been dealing with the after effects of the abortion for our whole marriage—so in a way, it's a welcome relief to find out she didn't have one. But I suppose I'm feeling a little anxious about telling our extended families. For obvious reasons, what happened some twenty-odd years ago isn't common knowledge."

"Understood. Well, let me go and check the patient out first. I don't even know if this is going to be a good time. Wait here."

A few moments later, Dr. Taylor stuck his head in the door and motioned for them to follow him.

"Hey, Sheriff," Lance said as the trio walked into his fabric-walled cubicle.

"Hello, Lance. How are you feeling?" A.J. asked the young, red-headed boy swaddled in hospital sheeting.

"Not as bad as I thought I would actually. My leg hurts,

and they won't give me anything for it until they know if I have to have it set surgically or not, but other than that," Lance shrugged, "I'm actually okay. Not like Ben. I heard he had to have surgery to repair a muscle or something."

"He did, but he's doing okay. His family is with him now," Dr. Taylor offered.

"Ah, family," Lance said wistfully.

"Lance, I'd like for you to meet my wife, Melanie." A.J. put his arm around her shaking frame.

"Hi."

"Hi, Lance. A.J.'s told me a lot about you. You were pretty brave back there."

"I don't know what the sheriff told you, but he must have been smokin' something. I was scared out of my wits."

"That's not what I heard, from him or from the girl you saved."

"Enin? Oh, she just thinks I was brave because I was a little less afraid than she was. Believe me, it was a weird experience. So do you work here or something?" Lance asked Melanie, trying to make some sense out of why she was in his room.

"Ah, no. I came down here . . ." Melanie rubbed her hands together as she first looked at A.J. and then at Dr. Taylor.

"Is there something going on here I need to know about?" Lance asked. "Hey, Enin's okay, right? Is it Ben? Blake? Jared?"

"No, no. This isn't about them. It's about you, or rather us," A.J. said.

"Us? Us who?"

"Well, 'us' as in you and I."

"Am I in some kind of trouble?"

"No. It's about your mother, Belinda," A.J. said in a voice so soft that Lance had to raise slightly from his pillow to understand the sheriff.

"Oka-a-a-y. . ." Lance said. He let the word draw out slowly until it faded into the sound barrier behind his bed.

"Remember when we were talking in the cave earlier tonight?"

"Yes," Lance said, his eyes narrowing and his head nodding.

"And remember how I said I dated her?"

"Yeah. Then you left for Mississippi or Missouri or somewhere like that."

"Missouri. Well, what I didn't say, or couldn't say, was that when I left your mother, she, well . . . " A.J. shut his eyes and continued, "She was pregnant."

Lance didn't say anything. He looked from the doctor standing over him, to the woman visibly shaking next to her husband, to the sheriff who was blindly chewing on his lower lip.

"Are you saying what I think you're saying?" Lance finally said.

"Maybe. What are you hearing?" A.J. said, opening his eyes but afraid to say the words out loud himself.

"Are you trying to tell me you think you're my dad? Is that what this is all about?"

There was silence from the three adults in the room.

"That's impossible. My mom told me my dad died. She said he was in the Gulf War and was killed." Lance's voice was rising with anxiety.

"Your mom told me she had an abortion. She never gave me a chance. Before I could even talk to her, she had written me to say she'd had an abortion. I was in Missouri. I never heard from her again."

"But . . ." Lance grabbed his mouth and closed his eyes. Tears squeezed out of both eyes in unison.

"Lance. I never knew. I swear." A.J.'s voice pleaded. "I stayed in the service for fifteen years. I didn't date, not after that. I couldn't—so I decided to be a career soldier. Only after my dad died and my mom needed me did I come back here. I met Melanie and we were married five years ago. We have six kids."

"Six kids? In five years?" Lance said, opening his eyes and raising his head again to look at A.J. and his wife.

They both stifled a nervous laugh when they saw the look on Lance's face.

"Yes," Melanie spoke. "Six children. Two are biological. Then we adopted twins from Korea and two black brothers from Ghana. A.J. told me about your mother when we were dating, of course, but neither of us knew about you. We never even suspected."

"Do you realize that if this is true that I now have something like eighteen siblings?"

"Well, this *is* Utah," Dr. Taylor said helpfully. A.J., Melanie and Lance turned to look at him through furrowed foreheads of surprise. Dr. Taylor shrugged and smiled.

"So what do we do now? Do you want my blood or something for DNA testing?" Lance said, breaking the silence.

Dr. Taylor looked at the Lanzes and smiled. "Smart kid. So much for my needed expertise."

"Uh, yeah, actually that's exactly what we were thinking. We'd pay for it, of course," A.J. said.

"Sheriff," Lance started his sentence.

"Look, I think it would be okay if you called me A.J."

"Okay, A.J." Lance stopped and tilted his head to the side. "Hey, what does A.J. stand for anyway?"

"Alma Jacob," A.J. said, looking Lance straight in the eye. "Or if you prefer, Alma Jacob Lanz."

"Alma Lanz? Alma Lanz! I'm Lance Alma!"

The words hung in the air, each person taking in the enormity of the situation. The quiet was palpable, which made the next thing they heard a thousand times louder than it probably was.

The sharp crack of gunfire in the hall brought the people in the room to full attention.

Chapter

34

By the time they pulled into the parking lot of the hospital, dawn was creeping over the horizon. In the gray blue light of morning, the man in the overalls and tie hurried toward the double doors of the emergency room.

A moment later, a male nurse exited the double doors with a wheelchair. The overalled Samaritan followed close behind. Together they helped Wayne into the chair. The nurse pushed the chair up the ramp toward admitting; the man followed.

"What's your name, sir?" the nurse asked after they were settled in the triage room.

"Uh, Wayne Roy."

The nurse wrote this down on his form. "Wayne, do you know what day it is?" He then turned to Wayne and flashed a penlight in both of his eyes in rapid succession. Wayne pulled his head back in pain and then closed both eyes reflexively. "Ah, day? I . . . uh . . . I . . . don't remember."

The nurse looked at the man in the overalls and then wrote something else down.

"Okay, Wayne, how about this? What year is this?"

Wayne relaxed and then smiled the briefest of smiles. "Nineteen ninety," he said, nodding his head.

"Nineteen ninety?" the nurse said, surprised.

Wayne pulled his eyebrows together, confused at the nurse's response. "Yeah, I think so. I know I've been out of the country and all, but I ought to know what year it is."

"Okay," the nurse said and wrote something else down. He then turned to the man in the suit. "Where did you say you found him?"

"He was standing in the middle of the highway about half a mile down from Lone Oak Campground."

"Wayne," the nurse said, turning back to his charge, "where have you been? You said you'd been out of the country."

"Yeah, over in Iraq, trying to get that dirty . . ." he used an ugly word, "Saddam Hussein."

"You just got back from Iraq? I thought they got Saddam last year."

Wayne looked confused. "What? No, he's still out there. I ought to know. President Bush would have pulled us all out earlier if we had."

"George W.? No, we're still there. Too many insurgents making a mess of things for us to come home yet," the nurse said.

"Who's George W.?" Wayne said, putting his hand on the side of his head and kneading gently.

"George W. Bush," the man in the overalls answered.

"President Bush's son? Now why the heck would a Texas governor be involved in the Gulf War?"

The nurse and old man looked at each other startled.

"Mr. Roy doesn't have any ID?" the nurse asked after a moment.

"No."

The nurse looked at Wayne, who was staring off into space,

and then at the man in the overalls. "Yeah, I guess. Well, looks like we need to get Mr. Roy here seen. Let me see what we can do. It's a little busy right now. They brought in a kid with a gunshot a bit ago. Things are a little crazy back there. Wayne is disoriented for sure but not in any real danger yet. I'll see if I can find him a bed."

A few minutes later, the nurse returned, a frown on his face.

"Looks like Wayne's going to have to sit in the waiting room a bit, or we can send you to a different hospital emergency room. We're full to capacity right now with two more ambulances on the way. Can you keep an eye on him? Let me know if his condition changes at all."

"Sure I can. I just need to call the missus first. I was on my way to pick up some feed for the store. She'll be wondering what happened to me."

"I'll stay with Wayne while you call," the nurse offered.

When the man returned five minutes later, Wayne was sitting alone in the waiting room. The man shrugged and sat down beside him.

"What happened to the nurse?" he asked.

Wayne Roy was watching an *I Love Lucy* rerun on the black institutional television hanging from the ceiling. He crooked his head and looked at the man; then he turned it back to watch Lucy put something in the oven.

The old man shook his head and picked up a magazine.

Wayne Roy alternately watched the television and winced in pain. The man looked at his watch every time Wayne Roy jumped. The pains were pretty regular, whatever that might mean. They sat in the empty waiting room for over an hour. Finally the older man rose.

"You stay here, buddy. I'm going to talk to that dang nurse again. You don't look so good."

Wayne didn't answer—he only rocked back and forth in his wheelchair.

"Better yet, you come with me. This just ain't right."

The man gripped the handles of the wheelchair and moved it purposefully toward the triage room again.

Amazingly, no one was in triage. The man pushed the wheelchair in one door and then out the opposite door into the emergency room. There were half a dozen medical personnel scurrying around.

"Hey there," the man said to a young female walking by. "This here man needs a doctor."

"I'm sorry, sir, I'm just a secretary. Let me find you someone. What room are you in?"

"Ain't in no room," the man said impatiently. "That there's the problem."

The young girl looked puzzled, "I'm sorry. Not in a room?"

"Nope, he ain't been seen by a doctor yet."

"Well then, how'd you get back here?" she said, looking toward the triage room down the hall.

"Just came on back through that little room in the front."

"Oh. Well, wait right here. I'll go get the triage nurse," she said a bit nervously and headed down the hall.

The man didn't want to wait. He pushed a moaning Wayne down the hall, following slowly behind her. He stopped when she went into a room. He noticed Wayne cock his head as he looked into an exam room on his left.

Then Wayne bent over and looked like he was rubbing his calves.

The next thing the man knew, Wayne had a gun in his hand, and he was aiming it straight into the exam room.

"Hey, buddy," the old farmer said excitedly to Wayne. "What's going . . ." But before he could complete his sentence, Wayne had fired one shot and then another. The lights flickered and went out.

Chapter

35

It only took one second for Enin to register who was being pushed past the open door of her exam room. He was in a hospital issue wheelchair. He was pressing a mottled red, wadded up mass of gauze to his face. She didn't recognize the middle-aged man in overalls and a tie who gently moved him past the half dozen or so full-to-capacity exam rooms, but by the time her hand flew to cover her open mouth, Crazy Guy had recognized her. She saw him bend over and lift one of the flaps on the lower left leg of his faded camouflaged pants. She remembered what was in that pocket; she had seen him put it there while they were riding in the Taurus. She backed into the room, knocking over the crash cart and spilling the once-sterilized paraphernalia over the linoleum floor.

The first shot from the Glock hit the glass in the exam cabinet above the sink. Once shattered, the acrid smell of alcohol and benadine filled the air. Drizzling down from the broken bottles, the wound cleansers mixed and pooled into an inky-rust colored mess on the Formica countertop and then cascaded over the edge and splashed the remaining thirty-two inches to the floor.

The screaming came next. Guttural and high at the same time, Enin wasn't sure if it was coming from inside or outside of her brain. She thought of Ben and Lance down the hall. She was sure they would be next. She whispered their names, a plaintive prayer for their safety.

The second shot pierced through the wall near the light switch. The lights in her room flickered and then died. The whole of the emergency room went dark for what seemed like an eternity. Then the backup lights came on, bathing the room in a light just low enough to make out the shape of someone at her door. In the soft focus, she saw him standing with his gun aimed directly at her.

A third shot was fired, and they both crumpled to the ground.

Chapter

36

The sharp crack of the first shot brought the whole department to a confused standstill, but only for a moment. At the sound of the second shot, doors slammed, people screamed, trash cans were knocked over under desks where secretaries took cover.

In Lance's room, A.J. pushed his wife down. Dr. Taylor threw himself over Lance, who winced in response, and A.J. drew his gun, heading for the open door.

In Ben's room, his father got up and slammed the door shut.

In the interior family waiting room, people screamed and held each other.

The lights went out, then on again, but with much less illumination. A.J. peered down the hall only to see panicked staff running toward him, giving him the general location of the trouble. He headed upstream, gun drawn. The river of people parted for the uniformed sheriff.

"He's got a gun," a nurse screamed redundantly in passing.

A.J. reached the end of the hall and peered around the corner. He saw a man in a wheelchair rise and stretch out his arms, aiming his pistol into one of the rooms.

A.J.'s years of military and police training kicked into high gear. Without a moment of hesitation or guilt, he aimed to kill.

The single shot hit the man in camouflaged pants, penetrating his right side between his arm and shoulder blade. He crumpled to the linoleum floor. An older man in overalls stood nearby, his back up against the wall opposite the open door.

"Drop!" A.J. shouted at the man.

The man slowly turned his head toward A.J. in confusion.

"I said *drop now*," A.J. repeated, aiming his gun directly at his tie.

The older man dropped in a dead faint.

A.J. walked on cat paws toward the two men on the floor. He kicked the Glock away from the body on the floor and then cuffed the bleeding and barely breathing man in the doorway of the exam room. He glanced in the room to see what he had been shooting at, but the room looked empty.

He cuffed the older man in overalls, who was beginning to stir. By that time, a few curious faces of the security staff were peering around the corners of the halls.

"Someone get Dr. Taylor," he yelled.

A face backed into the hall, and he heard steps leaving the area.

"Is there anyone else?" he asked the onlookers.

"I don't think so," a young man in scrubs said and came tentatively around the corner toward A.J. "They came in together. The older guy on the floor said he found the guy in camos out on a highway. He said the guy in the camos had been in a car accident and was just standing in the middle of the road."

"That's correct, Officer," the older man said out of the side of his mouth, his cheek still kissing the cold linoleum floor. "He hit a deer. He was pretty messed up."

"Did you see what he was driving?" A.J. said, though he was pretty sure he already knew the answer to this question.

"I never saw the car myself, but he said his Taurus hit a deer. First time I saw him he was standing in the middle of the road. Scared the poop right out of me. I almost hit him myself."

A.J. put his gun back in its holster and used a hankie from his pocket to pick up the Glock on the floor. A.J. then moved closer to the old farmer on the floor and bent down. He cut off the zip-tie he had been handcuffed with and helped the gentleman to his feet.

Dr. Taylor was coming down the hall, taking in the situation. "I take it this is the shooter," he said, looking down at the guy in camos that people seemed to mostly be ignoring.

A.J. nodded his head. "How are Melanie and Lance?"

"Shook up naturally, but okay. Lance keeps asking about Enin."

"Where is Enin?" A.J. asked.

"She was in there a few minutes ago," Dr. Taylor said pointing to the exam room.

"I didn't see anyone in that room," A.J. said.

Dr. Taylor stepped over the body and entered the dimly lit room. Crunching on the broken glass under his Nikes, he didn't see anyone at first. Then tucked in a corner next to the exam bed, he saw a young girl sitting with her back to the far wall.

"You okay?" Dr. Taylor said, surprised at her presence.

"I guess I'm okay. I'm not shot or anything, if that's what you mean. I think I may have fainted though. Is that guy gone? I mean, no offense, but is he dead or something?"

Dr. Taylor looked at the guy in the doorway. "I expect he is."

Enin nodded slowly. "Is it bad to want someone dead?" she asked.

"Not when that guy was trying to kill you. I think that's normal," Dr. Taylor answered gently as he held out his hand toward her.

She nodded her head. "Can I see my parents now?"

Dr. Taylor motioned for one of the nurses looking in the door to come over.

"Take her to Ben Woodson's room," Dr. Taylor said. Then he helped Enin step over the body in the doorway.

A.J. was startled to see Enin exit the room. He looked at Dr. Taylor who was gently helping support Enin.

"I had no idea," A.J. said finally.

"She fainted and was in the corner." A nurse offered Enin her own arm for support. She needs to be with her parents for now."

A.J. nodded his approval, though he would have to go and question her in a bit. He stepped out of their way.

After Enin was walking down the hall, Dr. Taylor bent down to examine the guy lying in an expanding puddle of blood. He put two fingers on his carotid artery and then shook his head at A.J.

A.J. shrugged, thinking about death, his son, and paperwork—in that order.

Chapter

37

"Ben!" Enin said breathlessly when she saw her brother lying in his hospital bed. Her mother and father ran to the open door, wrapping her in warm, loving arms.

"What was that all about?" her father said.

"It was that crazy guy. Somehow he ended up in the hospital too."

"What crazy guy?" her mother said.

"The one who kidnapped me and shot Ben."

Her mother's eyes widened, and she reached for a chair, backing herself into it.

"What was he shooting at now?" Ben said, motioning with his good arm for Enin to come to him.

"Me," she said as she crossed the room toward his bed.

"What?" her family said in unison.

Enin just shook her head in disbelief as well.

"I know. I was waiting in that exam room for a social

worker or someone like that, and he got pushed passed my room in a wheelchair. He saw me, and the next thing I knew he was pointing a gun through the door. I actually don't remember much after he shot the medicine cabinet. I fainted."

"Enin, are you all right?" her mother gasped, the words packed with meaning.

Enin took Ben's hand; then he looked from her mom to her dad to her gathering family in the doorway. "I'm surprisingly okay. I remember being more worried about Ben and Lance when I first saw the gun, but then I fainted and the rest is a blank. I think I was being protected from above from both physical as well as mental harm."

Enin's extended family gathered around her and Ben. They had entered the room silently but then began to speak all at once. It was music to Enin's ears.

"This has been some night, huh?" Ben said over the din of voices. His good hand still held Enin's.

Enin squeezed his in response.

Ben motioned with his head for Enin to come closer. She bent down, and he started to whisper. She moved even closer until his warm breath tickled her ear.

"Enin, you're my hero. You always have been."

"Don't be . . ." Enin started to say, but Ben cut her off with a "shush."

"Just listen for a second." He lowered his voice even more. "I was wrong. You were right. I needed Heavenly Father, and I shut him out as much as I shut you and Mom and Dad out. I was crazy after Mandy got married, but lately I've been thinking, really hard actually, and every time you came over, all sweetness and light, and took care of me in spite of my rudeness I hurt even more. How could you have such faith I wondered, and what had happened to mine? Well, little by little I've been coming around. I talked to Sister Parker yesterday."

"Yeah, I heard. Lance told me," Enin whispered back, still leaning over her brother.

"She died yesterday."

"What?" Enin backed away for a moment and looked her brother in the eye.

He nodded his head and then motioned for her to return to their private conversation.

"I know, it was a shock for me too. I was the last person to see her alive. Well, Lance and I, that is. Before she left, she gave me some good advice. The thing is, her advice wasn't anything different than what you've been telling me all along. I've been an idiot these past couple of years, and while I thought the only person I was hurting was myself, it turns out that was a lie. I've hurt you, Mom, and Dad. Heck, the whole family. What a jerk I've been," he said, shaking his head. His hair tickled Enin's face. "But I promise, it'll be different from now on. I'm even thinking of moving back home to save money for—well, whatever the future may bring."

Enin reached up a hand and brushed the side of Ben's face gratefully.

"I love you, Ben Woodson. Welcome home."

Chapter 38

Twenty minutes later, Enin entered Lance's room so softly that she hadn't made a sound, but Lance turned anyway. He felt her presence.

"Hey," he said.

"Hey to you too," Enin replied shyly.

"I heard about the shooting."

"Weird, huh?"

"Yeah, I'll say. How are you?"

"Okay, really. I fainted and I think that helped a lot. I missed most of the action, which is fine by me."

Lance nodded.

"So how are you?" Enin continued.

Lance smiled a crooked little smile that Enin couldn't read.

"What?" Enin said, puzzled.

"Well, I hear I have to go into surgery soon, but my father

is going to give me a blessing before I do, so I'll probably be okay."

"Your dad is here? Already? How the heck did he get here so fast?"

Lance smiled again.

"What? Why do you keep smiling like that? Are you on drugs or something?"

Lance laughed. "I wish. They haven't given me anything yet. They had to wait until they knew if I was going to have to have my leg set surgically first."

"Does your leg hurt?"

"A little when I move it."

"Okay, then why the heck do you keep smiling so weird?"

"I met my father—my real father," Lance said.

Enin shook her head in confused response.

"Not to be rude, but which father? Didn't you say you had a few?"

"Yes, I did. I said I had two stepdads and a father that had died."

"So who are we talking about here?"

"The father that died."

"You met your dead father?" Enin said, her brows furrowing.

"Exactly. Only he's not dead."

"All right, you have my attention."

"There is no simple way to say this, so just listen and hold your comments and questions for the end, okay?"

Enin nodded.

"When I was in the cave and Sheriff Lanz came in, we talked. It turned out he knew my mother from when he was in the marines and she worked on base. What I didn't know until I got to the hospital this morning was how *well* he knew her. They had been really close, and when he left, my mother was pregnant. My mother wrote and told him that she had had an abortion, so he never contacted her again."

"Are you saying . . ." Enin started.

Lance put a finger on her lips.

"So when he was with me in the cave, he figured it out, but he didn't say anything. He and his wife showed up in my hospital room and told me the whole thing. At first I was in shock. I mean, who wouldn't be? But then somehow I knew it was true. This whole trip to Utah was about finding my father, and you. . ." His voice trailed off.

"I can't believe it," Enin said at last.

Lance shrugged. "Nevertheless, it's true, and my dad is going to give me a blessing in a few minutes."

"I've heard about stuff like this happening but never to people I know. So what are you going to do?"

"I'm not entirely sure yet. I mean, it's not like I can just up and move in with this complete stranger. I guess I'll have to take it a little at a time. I have a feeling my stepdad and mom are going to be happy for me once they get over the shock. My stepmom is supposed to be here in a few hours."

"I talked to Ben."

"Oh, how is he? How's his arm?"

"He'll be okay. He already has been in and out of surgery. You were right about one thing though."

"What?"

"Well, he told me about meeting with Sister Parker yesterday."

"Who's Sister Parker?"

"Mandy's great-grandmother."

"Oh, so what was his version?"

"Pretty much the same as yours, and you were right. It really did affect him. He told me he was moving back home with our parents and that he is going to be going back to church. My mother is beside herself."

"I'll bet. And you? Do you think it's for real or just a reaction to his getting shot?"

"No, I think it's real. I think he really has had a change of heart. I could feel it."

Lance shrugged. "Me too. Like I said, I thought he was going to head straight for a bishop's house yesterday."

"So what about you?"

"What about me?"

"Have you had a change of heart?"

Lance turned his head away from her.

Enin touched his chin and pulled it back. Tears were in his eyes. Enin brushed them away with small gentle strokes from her fingers.

"That looks like a yes to me."

He nodded.

"This has been a weird weekend, hasn't it?"

"I'll say," Lance said, his voice full of emotion.

"Do you think you'll be staying in Utah?"

Lance nodded.

"I'd like that," Enin said, laying her head on his chest.

"I was hoping you would."

Epilogue

Magna est veritas, et praevalibit
(Truth is might and will prevail)

The chapel of the Magna Singles Ward was packed. While it sometimes happened, it wasn't often that three missionaries left at the same time for the same country.

The program listed Sister Enin Woodson as the first speaker, Elder Ben Woodson next, who was followed by Elder Alma Lance Lanz. The concluding speaker was Bishop Butler, who was at the pulpit now.

"A year ago this week, I met Elder Lanz after his truck was broken into. Of course, I knew Sister Woodson and Elder Woodson a long time prior to that. Over the course of this past year, I have been impressed by the dedication of these three young people in getting their lives arranged in order to serve the Lord on a full-time basis.

"It is no accident on the part of the Lord that they are all going to be serving in Brazil. He recognizes talents in us that we often overlook. Sister Woodson will bring her love and enthusiasm for the gospel; Elder Woodson, his incredible perception of the Book of Mormon; and Elder Lanz, his deep understanding of the principles of eternal families to the people of three different missions in Brazil.

"Over this past year, I have counseled with each of them on numerous occasions. Their desires to serve are sincere and their testimonies strong. They each love the Lord and have all been tested and found acceptable to do His work. We would do well to emulate them."

As the bishop spoke, A.J. held Melanie's hand. This day was a miracle on many levels. His son, who once was lost and now was found, was sitting on the stand in a dark suit. His countenance was serene. A.J. had been blessed to spend the last year getting to know this young adult. He found that Lance had many of the characteristics that had attracted him to Lance's mother in the first place. But Lance clearly was stronger than either he or Belinda Morris had ever been. Lance's testimony of the gospel was now deep and full. Once the decision to serve a mission had been made, he focused on that and nothing else—not even his budding relationship with Enin. He had put all things on hold until he returned, and Enin had been his biggest cheerleader since.

It wasn't a surprise to anyone when Enin put her papers in. It seemed natural. Everyone was mildly surprised that she had gotten called to Brazil, but not as much as when her brother got his call to Brazil as well. It was sweet and appropriate that they would all be in the MTC at the same time. The three of them had formed a very close relationship that would only deepen as a result of their respective callings.

A.J. scanned the faces on the stand. Such peace. It was hard to believe that a year ago they had all been struggling with the aftereffects of a deranged veteran.

A.J. still thought about Wayne Roy, the man he had killed. Wayne's life had been a tough one. After the Gulf War, he had been honorably discharged, but the gathering storm of mental illness overcame him. He had murdered a close army buddy, although that didn't come out until after he had been killed himself. He had been on medicine for severe depression and psychotic breaks for a few years before he kidnapped Enin.

The gun that Lance had found, along with the dog tags, belonged to the man Wayne Roy had murdered. They were able to locate his body and return it to the family, bringing at least a bit of closure to them.

As for A.J., he thought back to the day he'd gotten the letter from Belinda Morris, informing him of her decision to have an abortion. The anguish that he felt on that day had finally been totally quelled by the elation of this one.